Ronald J. Testa

LABOUR OF LOVE

Also by Peter McGehee

Boys Like Us
Sweetheart
Beyond Happiness: The Intimate Memoirs of Billy Lee Belle
The I.Q. Zoo (stories)

LABOUR OF LOVE

a novel by
Doug Wilson

based on characters created by
Peter McGehee

ST. MARTIN'S PRESS
NEW YORK

Library of Congress Cataloging-in-Publication Data

Wilson, Doug, d. 1992.
    Labour of love / Doug Wilson ; based on characters created by
Peter McGehee.
        p. cm.
    ISBN 0-312-09839-1
    1. Gay men—Ontario—Toronto—Fiction. 2. Family—Southern
States—Fiction. 3. AIDS (Disease)—Fiction. 4. Toronto (Ont.)—
Fiction. I. McGehee, Peter. II. Title.
PS3573.I456924L3 1993
813'.54—dc20   93-25737
                                                                      CIP

First Edition: November 1993

10 9 8 7 6 5 4 3 2 1

ACKNOWLEDGMENTS

Special thanks to Nancy Wilson, Gail van Varseveld, Bruce Martin, Jeanette Lavigne, Darien Taylor, and Elizabeth Philips, the first readers of the work; to Jeffrey for his constant confidence in this dream; and to all of the loved ones, everywhere, who have seen me through this terrible and wonderful time.

Thanks also to the Saskatchewan Writers' Colony for retreat time.

AUTHOR'S NOTE

Peter McGehee, my lover and longtime companion, died from complications related to AIDS in September 1991. His novel *Boys Like Us* had appeared earlier that year. The second book of what he had always envisioned as a trilogy, *Sweetheart*, was in the publishing process when he died. It was released in the spring of 1992.

Shortly after Peter's death, I discovered a brief note outlining the time period of an unnamed third novel—a novel he would never write.

As editor of all Peter's published work, his literary executor, and his creative collaborator for more than twelve years, I have undertaken to write that third book. Finish the trilogy he dreamed of. Complete the circle.

To do so, I have used many of the characters developed in the first two books. And have added others. I have also shifted the narrative voice. Zero MacNoo's longtime friend and companion, David, takes up the tale.

Labour of Love, like the other two novels, may be read independently, in sequence, or out of sequence, with its companion titles.

CONTENTS

LABOUR OF LOVE

PERFORMING WITHOUT A NET

It's seven in the morning. I hear the first sounds of activity upstairs. He's been getting up earlier and earlier, since Jeff died. Since his own health really started to slide. Since he started the second novel.

He begins tapping at his laptop. I finish my crossword, then put on the coffee. Five minutes later, two steaming mugs in hand, I slowly climb the stairs to his flat. "Zero," I call, "you ready for java?"

"Come on in," he says. "Don't leave the door open. I find it chilly in here lately. I'll have to speak to the landlord."

"I am your landlord."

"Precisely," he replies, grinning weakly. He's sprawled in front of his desk in his robe, unshaven, unshowered. He doesn't look well.

"Bad night?"

"Yeah, high fever again. Headache. How about you?"

I groan. "I was up most of the night with this damn diarrhea. I'm wasted. No wonder cryptosporidium is often fatal. I've lost fifty pounds over the course of a year and a half. It's too much and I just can't stop it. It's like my body is eating itself. I'm disappearing."

He rummages among the papers on his desk. "Well, there's something here in Project Inform you might want to show to Dr. Fieldstone when you're out to the hospital next. It's called Humatin

3

and they say it's worked against crypto for some people. Very experimental, though."

I take the newsletter. "Thanks." I turn to go. I know his work pattern. Several hours of solid writing first thing every morning. Except for this coffee.

"David, can you sit down with me for a while?"

"Sure, Zero. What's up?"

"Not much these days." He manages a smile. "What are we gonna do, David? We're both sicker than dogs. I have holes in my brain, and you're wasting away. What happens the day neither one of us can do for the other?"

"I think we passed that day awhile ago."

"Sure we've managed so far, but who's going to look after us later on?"

"Ourselves. Each other. Our friends. Like so much of our lives now, we'll just make it up as we go along. Perform without a net." I do a little dance for him. "How am I doing so far?"

"I wish I had your confidence." He sips his coffee. "You know, if something were to happen to you, I have nightmares of my mother coming up here to take care of me. That would kill me. Or, worse yet, of her carting me back to Arkansas. Quite frankly, I'd sooner kill myself." He shudders.

"Zero, we'll be fine."

"Don't pollyanna me, David."

"What am I supposed to say?"

"Don't say anything, just come here and give me a hug." He staggers slightly as he stands up. I hold him tight against me. I feel wetness on my neck. He's weeping.

"Damn this life!" he cries. "Just when it starts to go your way they pull the rug out from under you. It makes me so fucking angry, and so fucking sad."

"But some good things have happened, Zero. Your first novel

has been a great success. It looks like you're coming right along on the second. You have fans and friends. You've got me."

"I know all that, David, but I'm dying. I really do have holes in my brain and, even though it's been nearly a year, I miss Jeff terribly. And Randy. And all the others."

"I still can't believe that Jeff is gone. You must miss him so."

"Oh, I do . . . but in so many ways it seems like he was a dream. He was here, then gone. A quick, sweet memory."

"Still, it must be hard . . ."

"Of course, but in many ways I was just getting to know him. It's not like losing Randy, or if I were to lose you."

"Why?"

"Time, I guess. You've been in my life for more than twelve years. You're so much of my history. Rooted in all my memories, good and bad. And you've loved me through it all. I know that and I couldn't bear to lose it."

"But you might. One of us is going to go first, Zero."

"I know, David, I know."

He turns away and picks up his coffee. "Come out on the deck. The yellow hibiscus is blooming."

The deck is still kind of cool. There isn't much out there. "Don't you think it's a little early to have the hibiscus out?" I ask.

"I wanted them to catch some morning light."

"Oh, that's probably okay."

Jeff built Zero a beautiful garden on this deck last spring, and Zero, who in all our years together had never shared my gardening enthusiasm, developed a passion for it, particularly after Jeff's death.

We stand in the morning sun. There is a breeze. It smells like spring. I slip my arm around him. "You know, Zero, this is getting harder. Just physically, the stairs, the cleaning, laundry. I've been reluctant to suggest it, but why don't you just think about moving downstairs again? We could make up your old office into a bedroom for you. We could . . ."

He's quiet a moment. "No, David."

"No? As in no way?"

"No, I meant it wouldn't be necessary to set up my old room. I want to be able to curl up with you again. I really need you now."

I turn and wrap him in my thinning arms once more. "Well, if you're sure."

"I'm very sure."

"Okay then. I'll put some ads up around and see if I can get some good bodies to move in up here. We can have a moving party on the weekend. In the meantime, I'll shift the office around so we can both work like before. Sound okay?"

"Sounds great." He kisses me on the forehead. "Now get outa here. I'm trying to write."

I go back downstairs. I gather the papers spread out on the kitchen table and take them back to the office. There won't be much to rearrange back here. When Zero moved out so suddenly a couple of years ago, I just filled the spot where his desk had been with plants. And my inevitable stacks of paper. I guess I always knew he'd be back. Hoped anyway.

Except for those few months away with Clay, and his more recent stay upstairs, he and I have lived together for more than twelve years. It has been hard having him away. We have grown together. And this house has been our home for a long time.

When we moved to Toronto from out West we crammed all of our worldly goods into one small room above Novak's Pharmacy at Church and Wellesley. I hadn't come to Toronto with any intention of being a home owner. Who could afford it? Getting this house on Maitland had been pure luck.

Performing Without a Net

I met the owner, an old German immigrant, in a local bar one day. Trax, I think it was. We struck up a lively conversation and over the course of several meetings we became good friends. He had been a hobo for much of his life, always chasing the next train out of town. Riding the rails wherever they would take him. In many ways he was a lonely old guy, but full of wild and wonderful yarns. He insisted on calling himself a hobosexual. I thought he was delightful.

I had him over to share our first Christmas dinner in Toronto. He got uproariously drunk, donned a platinum blond wig, and crooned Dietrich songs for hours. After midnight I walked him home down Church Street. On the doorstep of the rambling old house on Maitland, where I guess I just assumed he rented a room, he kissed me and quoted Hebrews 13.2: "Be not forgetful to entertain strangers, for thereby some have entertained angels unawares."

A week and a half after New Year's, a lawyer called me. Erick had died in his sleep and left me this house. It's been my home, our home, ever since.

I call Searcy. "Searce, I've convinced Zero to move back downstairs."

"Thank goodness. Was it a struggle?"

"No, surprisingly."

"Well, when do we move him?"

"How about eleven on Saturday? Can you call Snookums for me?"

"Sure, I'll round up some other little helpers as well."

"You are a doll! Oh, also, if you hear of anybody looking for a two-bedroom apartment, let me know. They could move in anytime."

"Sure thing. I'll spread the word. I've gotta run to a 'Gong Show' audition now. No time to tarry. I'll call you later."

LABOUR OF LOVE

* * *

I'm heading home about dusk. At the corner by the Queen's Dairy a hatchback crammed with young hosers slows down beside me. One of the kids mouths "faggot!" at me through the back window. Straight boys in from the 'burbs looking for trouble. I hope they don't linger in the neighborhood. They seem to be headed over to Yonge Street. I'm about to turn up Maitland when an unmistakable figure emerges from the alley behind the Superfresh. Searcy. I see him just as the kids see him. One of them shouts at him from an open window. Searcy gives him a bejeweled finger. They immediately slam on their brakes and pile out of the car. "Get the fat faggot!" one yells. There are five of them. They are around him in an instant. Kicking. Throwing punches. He goes down. Hard.

I am frozen. Immobilized. I scream, "Searcy!" I turn to run back. "Gay bashers on Maitland!" I shout to startled people on Church. I pull out my alarm whistle. A couple of others do the same.

Searcy is sprawled on the sidewalk. You can hear the dull thud of boots connecting with flesh and their ugly cursing as they crowd around him. My face is wet with tears. I call his name again and again. It's not far but it seems like I'm running under water. Like I'll never get there. What I intend to do when I get there I have no idea. The air begins to fill with the sound of alarm whistles. "They're killing him!" I cry.

And then, incredibly, he's on his feet. He's bloody and his clothes are torn but he moves like a dancer. And he is angry. "You little scum-sucking sonafabitches!" he bellows. He picks up the nearest one by the scruff of the neck and the crotch and pitches him howling right over the hatchback into the center of the street. The kid lies still. Searcy is about to pitch another one when about eight of us arrive and face the others down. Soon the kids are ringed by angry folks from the neighborhood. The punk in the road is just beginning to stir and his buddies are a frightened lot. They huddle together, pale, sullen, and silent. The crowd is ugly. Searcy is being ministered to by some of the kitchen staff from Pints across the road.

Finally, the police arrive. They gather information, snap their little notebooks shut, and, without arresting anyone, turn to go. The crowd is thunderstruck. We gather around the squad car. Searcy is on his feet again.

"What the hell is going on here?" he roars.

The young woman who seems to be in charge says, "Everything seems to be under control here, sir."

"Under control!" Searcy is incredulous. "I am attacked on the street in my own neighborhood. They call me names and try to kill me and you think this is under control? If my friends and neighbors hadn't come along I could be dead. No, this isn't under control until charges are laid and you get these freaks arrested and out of here."

The cop is furious, but polite. "The situation is finished, sir. Now, we are very busy . . ." She turns to go.

"Listen, sister, you're finished when charges are laid." Searcy steps between her and the squad car.

The crowd, which has grown, takes up the cry. "Lay charges! Lay charges!" There is a momentary standoff as two more police cars screech up. After a hurried and heated discussion among the cops, charges are laid and the bashers are carted away to jeers and whistles from the crowd.

Searcy is the man of the hour. Bloody and battered, but triumphant. He leans heavily against me. His eyes are very tired.

A young man with green hair jumps up on the top of the bashers' car. He's wearing a Queer Nation button. "Join us here next Saturday at three P.M. for a rally to protest bashing and to celebrate this successful defense of our neighborhood," he enjoins the crowd.

I and a couple of the bar staff from Woody's help Searcy up the street to my place. Zero's light is off. He must already be asleep. People cheer as we mount the steps.

"Thanks boys," I say.

LABOUR OF LOVE

* * *

Searcy is quiet. Inside, I sit him down and make tea. When I turn back to him he's crying. "I am so frustrated and angry," he sobs. "So goddamned angry. Here we are in one of the largest lesbian and gay communities in the world. We provide so much of the heart of this town, yet the cops and the city let us be beaten and even killed in our own neighborhood. Something's got to be done."

"What, Searcy? We've demonstrated; we've lobbied. There've been some changes, some real solid ones, but in a lot of ways nothing's changed."

"We need to take it further. We need to let them know we won't take it anymore."

Later, I hear Zero moving around upstairs. I phone. "Are you okay up there?"

"Sure. I was asleep for a while, but my fever's spiking again."

"Can I help?"

"Bring me up some Advil, if you have any."

I find the bottle and take it up. He's sitting there in his T-shirt and boxers. I go directly to the sink and get a glass of water. I kiss him before I hand him the pills. He's burning up. I tell him about Searcy's bashing. He hadn't heard the chanting or the whistles.

"Damn them," he says.

"Damn who?" I ask.

"The fag bashers, the cops, homophobes everywhere."

He lays his head on my shoulder. I cuddle him into the crook of my arm. In seconds he's asleep and soon so am I. I wake up hours later. We are propping each other up on the sofa. My arm is totally numb. I ease it slowly out from behind him. He's cool now and undisturbed by my movement. I lay him out full length on the couch, get a blanket, and tuck him in. I let myself out, quietly.

Performing Without a Net

* * *

Saturday morning is glorious. The air is full and fresh with spring. I'm anxious to get at my garden, but today Zero moves downstairs and this afternoon is the antiviolence demo. That seems like quite a full day to me. I'm learning to pace myself. It isn't easy. The phone rings.

"David," Zero croaks, "bring up the coffee pronto." He sounds awful.

"Yes, your highness," I reply.

He greets me at the door with a kiss. "Thank goodness," I say, "you sounded wretched on the phone."

"I was, but now that I'm actually up I feel okay. What time are they coming?"

"Eleven."

"It's really sweet of you to let me move back in," he says.

"I never wanted you to leave in the first place," I reply. "You've been my true love since the moment we met. I know you needed fresh romance and passion in your life. It did hurt that you thought you had to move out to get it.

"I've always done a good job of looking after myself, but I also realized that we were a unit. Come rain, or come shine, I was with you for the duration. So, love, I was here, and I always wanted you to be, too."

"That's what I fucking hate about you, David. You're too damn perfect." He pauses. "It's what I love about you, too."

We read the Saturday paper together. He goes for the entertainment section, the headlines, Miss Manners, and, for some strange reason, the business report. Business I never read, but otherwise I'm a cover-to-cover man with the crossword as dessert.

Snookums is the first to arrive. He looks a little drawn but claims it's because his turban is wound too tight.

"Loosen it up," Zero counsels.

"Too much trouble, precious. There are miles of material in these damn things and it's no picnic getting it tied in the first place."

"Maybe you should try one of those turban jobs à la Gloria Swanson," suggests Zero.

"Now that's not a bad idea."

We can hear Searcy on the street below. It sounds like he's greeting and being greeted by everyone he meets. We hear him check downstairs to see where we are then begin his thunderous assault on the stairway.

"Yoo hoo! Darlings! I'm here! I do so wish we still had sedan chairs. I swear I'd have myself carted everywhere by a six-pack of burly youths."

"How are you feeling?" Zero is all concern.

"Not bad, hon. Lots of bruises, none, fortunately, on my fabulous face. Doctor Garth says I really am lucky. I could very easily have sustained broken bones, a concussion, and internal injuries. As luck would have it, under all my bangles and beads I have the body of a buffalo. That's more than those cowards ever count on. I keep thinking though, what if they had set upon you, Zero, or David? You guys would have been kicked to pieces in your present condition. The more I think about it the more furious I become. I'm tired of us being fair game. It's got to end."

"But how, Searcy, how?" Zero asks shaking his head.

"Well, my chicks, some of the local New Democratic activists have approached me to seek the party's nomination for City Council here in Ward Six in the November election. I know it seems farfetched, but what do you think?"

"Do you think you could win, precious?" asks Snookums.

"More to the point, could you do anything?" is my question.

"Yes, and yes," Searcy replies. He's obviously been thinking about this. "I'm already the reigning diva on the bar scene, and have been for quite some time, I might add. I'm probably the only one who can mobilize that crowd. My record of service in the community is solid. I'm now a saint of the Queer Nation crowd, and since the newspaper coverage of my battle with the bashers, everyone in my building and on the street seems to think I'm some kind of hero. Besides, I have oodles of personality, and lots and lots of fabulous outfits. It could be one of the great performances of my life," he concludes breathlessly.

I shake my head. "I don't know, Searcy, it's hard stuff, demeaning, and full of compromises."

"A lot like life in general, eh, David?" Snookums chuckles.

"Sounds like showbiz to me," adds Zero.

"Well, Searcy, if there's anything I can do, I'm at your command," declares Snookums.

"Thanks, Snooks, I knew I could count on you."

"Me, too," chimes in Zero. "Don't know what I can do, but I'll do anything."

"What about you, David? You're the one I need the most, with all your contacts and organizing experience."

I let him wait a few seconds. "It's a great idea, Searcy, I'll do all I can," I say, giving him a hug. He winces and then beams.

"David and I are pretty wimpy though, these days," reminds Zero.

"I know that, hon, but I just couldn't contemplate this without knowing that the two of you were involved in some way."

"You should approach Millie Gobert upstairs," I suggest. "She used to be one of the best political organizers in the whole country. She'd probably jump at the chance." My head is already full of possibilities. "Listen, Searcy, let's get Zero moved and go to the demo. I'll give this some thought and maybe we can get an organizing meeting together next week. There's some people I need to call."

LABOUR OF LOVE

"Oh, wonderful! I knew, if you were to get on it, David, it would get organized," Searcy enthuses.

"Remember though, I just don't have a lot of extra energy these days."

"I know, hon, believe me, I know."

Three strapping young men appear at the door.

"Well, let's get this princess moved," booms Searcy. "I have arranged with Brent, Blaine, and Bob from Woody's to be our moving surrogates since my old carcass is still a mass of aches and pains, and Zero and David are so frail."

"I, myself, am quite able-bodied," volunteers Snookums. He smiles vivaciously at Blaine, the tallest of the three. "Let's get at it."

It doesn't take long. Zero had moved out with very little of his stuff, and salvaged even less when he left Clay. It's really mostly just a question of books, computer, clothes, and a few cooking utensils.

It's just after noon. One of us has decided to run for political office, Zero has moved back into his home, and I now have an empty flat to rent.

Searcy and I make lunch.

Zero stretches out for a nap, sighing, "Oh, how I've missed this bed."

Bob and Brent need to get back to work, but Blaine and Snookums disappear upstairs to straighten up the newly vacated apartment. They reappear about twenty minutes later. They are both a trifle flushed. Snookums's turban is askew.

"Poltergeists?" inquires Searcy sweetly.

"Gotta get back to work now," says Blaine, blushing. "Later, guys. I'll call you after my shift, Snookums. Okay?"

"Sure, precious," Snookums replies, with a dreamy smile.

Performing Without a Net

"Thanks for all the help," we chorus.

"Well, sister," says Searcy. "What have you been up to? You could give yourself a heart attack carrying on in this manner. Not to mention the wear and tear on me, just thinking about it."

"He is lovely," says Snookums, "but too young. I'm in the market to marry, not adopt."

"Heartbreaking," says Searcy shaking his head.

Zero sleeps through lunch. I'll feed him something hot later on, before the demo. He's never been a great fan of demonstrations, but he is intent on being at this one.

He takes my arm as we head to the corner. We can hear the chanting and whistle blowing up at the Second Cup where the marchers have assembled. We wait for them at the corner. It's a motley, raucous crew, exuberant in the spring sunshine. Many greet us. On the spot where Searcy was attacked, we rally. The speeches are vociferous, articulate, too long.

"They remind me of us fifteen years ago," I muse.

"Maybe I remember it wrong," replies Zero, "but I don't think they're having as much fun."

Searcy is met with sustained applause. He recounts the details of his bashing, calls for real solutions, then tells them he's been asked to run for City Council to try to make those solutions happen. People go wild. The shout goes up, "Searcy Goldberg! Searcy Goldberg!" then, "No more shit!"

I shake my head. "A star is born."

"Once again," Zero adds.

We spend the rest of the afternoon shifting things around to accommodate Zero's return. After dinner, he disappears back into the office and emerges with a stack of paper bound with a heavy rubber band.

LABOUR OF LOVE

"Could you read this for me?"

I'm astounded. I've edited all of his work through the years. The collection of columns that was printed in 1989, the second collection due out this fall, his first novel, which came out to such success earlier this year. But he's been so ill that even with his relentless daily work I had no idea he was so close to completing something else.

"I needed to at least finish this," he says. "There's so little time." His face is very tired and hopeful and proud.

"I can't wait to read it," I exclaim. I take it from him. He staggers slightly. "Shall we call it a day?"

"I think we better."

As I put out the light, he moves to fit himself against me in our old, tight, familiar knot. I feel completed again. Whole. I have missed this so much. Too much. He leans over to kiss me.

"Sweet dreams," I murmur, "welcome home."

The diarrhea rips through me all night. By morning I'm totally shaken and wasted. Zero seems to sleep soundly through my constant comings and goings. I start to read the manuscript. It's wonderful. Rich, funny, heartbreaking, wise. About six o'clock the codeine I take to control my guts kicks in. I read on, but am having trouble keeping my eyes open. I switch out the light and slip beneath the covers.

When I wake up he's propped up on his elbow watching me. "Good morning, did you sleep well?" I ask.

"Like a baby. You were up a lot, though."

"Yeah, it's crazy, but what can you do? I've tried everything to control this stuff."

"Well, ask Dr. Fieldstone about that Humatin I told you about. Do you have an appointment this week?"

"On Tuesday. If I don't disappear before then. Damn it, Zero. Over fifty pounds in the last eighteen months! I have to put the brakes on this somehow."

Performing Without a Net

"I didn't realize it was so much. You still look pretty good."

"Yeah, I've got really attractive bones. It's not even being thin that's so bad. It's the constant terror of it. Many days I don't dare leave the house. When it's very bad I just don't feel human. I'm reduced to being a creature whose life is limited to within scampering distance of the nearest can," I complain.

"What a pair we've turned out to be," he says. "Who would have guessed that we would have ended up so soon as a pair of decrepit old crocks comparing our aches and pains before breakfast?"

"Who could have guessed any of this?" I reply.

Dr. Susan Fieldstone reads the article I've handed her on Humatin. "I don't know much about this one," she muses, "but I think I can get it for you under the Emergency Drug Release Plan. We might as well try it. Cryptosporidium can be fatal and you haven't responded to much else."

"How soon do you think we can get it?"

"Call me Friday morning."

A ray of hope.

"How's Zero?" she asks.

"I was going to ask you the same thing. He's moved back downstairs with me."

"Good. He's going to need you," she says, closing my bulging file.

"That file is alarming."

"In this business," she says with a tired smile, "the longer you live, the fatter the file. This just means you're one of my long-term survivors." She picks up the phone. "Call me Friday."

When I get back home Zero has gone out. He's written down some telephone messages but his handwriting is nearly indecipherable. I can read the numbers but can't figure out the names. His scrawl has seriously deteriorated in the last few days. I am filled with foreboding.

I am just stretching out, in an effort to get some sleep, when the phone rings. I debate letting the machine take it, but pick it up on the fourth ring. It's Mary Bull, the turkey baster–conceived daughter of Zero's late cousin, Trebreh. He was better known as porn star Billy Rockett. I'd met Mary Bull when she'd appeared on my doorstep a couple of years ago. Before she'd become a musical comedy star; before her dad had died with AIDS-related complications in L.A.

"Hi, David." She sounds anxious. "Do you know where Zero is? His phone's been disconnected. Has something happened?"

"He's moved back down here with me," I reply. "He's out right now. What's up?"

"What a relief! I was absolutely frantic when the operator said his phone was cut off."

"Where are you?"

"I'm back in New York City, and guess what, I've just signed a ten-month contract for a Broadway show!" she crows.

"That's wonderful, Mary Bull. Congratulations!"

"We start rehearsals in two weeks. It's called *Peanuts in the White House*. It's a musical about Jimmy Carter. I play Amy and I've got great songs!"

"Zero will be so proud. When do you open?"

"Mid-September, if all goes well. Will you guys come?"

"You know we wouldn't miss it for the world. Zero's going to be so excited."

"Well, that's my news. I have to run to class. Give Zero my love. Tell him I'll call soon. Do you have my New York number? Of course you don't!" She rattles it off. "You guys look after each other. Okay?"

I've been sleeping about an hour when I hear someone at the door. For a moment I'm disoriented. Who has keys? Just myself, Searcy, and

Lance. Could it be Lance? Then I remember—Zero's back. I sit up as he comes in.

"How'd it go at the hospital?" he asks.

"Not bad. She's going to get me that drug. Where have you been?"

"More lab work. Then I sat in Cawthra Park for a while. The big currant bush you told me about by the corner of the community centre is just beginning to bloom. It smells like heaven." He sits down heavily. "I'm exhausted and famished," he sighs.

"Why don't you lie down for a while, and if you feel like it we could go have a pizza at Bersani's in a bit."

"Good plan," he says, heading down the hall.

"Oh, Zero, Mary Bull phoned," I call after him. I give him her news.

He lights up. "That's great! Let's organize Snookums and Searcy and all go down for her opening. I'm going to book us flights first thing tomorrow morning."

"Fine with me," I respond.

"Did you see those other messages?" he asks.

"Couldn't read them, hon," I say cautiously, hoping not to offend him.

He sighs. "I was afraid of that. Anyway, there were three calls about the second-floor apartment. Let's see that note. The first one is Kirby, the second is Becky or something. Shit! I can't read the third at all. I think she said Frenchie. I was half asleep."

"Frenchie? As in Frenchie La Touche?" I ask.

"Frenchie La Touche? Do I know her?"

"Sure, but she was probably Olga Wrbinski then."

"Olga? Of course I know Olga. How did Olga become Frenchie? Or dare I ask?"

"I'm not sure. I haven't seen her since the Bermuda Triangle moved up to that farm near Parry Sound to live off the land. I think the story is that she found out she was adopted after nearly fifty years

19

of thinking her name was Olga Wrbinski. So she tracked down her birth parents. Her real name, it turns out, is something real dull, like Mary Smith. She was appalled at the banality of it, and I guess decided to take her destiny into her own hands. She'd been a stripper years ago at the Zanzibar Tavern on Yonge Street, so she decided to go back to her old stage name. Says it gives her a touch of class.

"I wonder if she's really interested in the apartment by herself or if it's for the entire trio? Either way would be great."

"Well, whatever her name is today, it'd be great if they're interested. Now I'm going to lie down before I fall down." Zero yawns.

I pick up the phone and dial the third number.

The Bermuda Triangle is an unholy trinity of lesbians, Hoo Hoo, Lucy Culpepper, and the notorious Frenchie. They had teamed up in the late 1970s in some sort of inexplicable ménage à trois. Over the years so many lesbians had come to grief on the rocks and shoals of this three-headed relationship that some waggish dyke had labeled them the Bermuda Triangle. The name had stuck.

I've worked on scores of projects with them over the years, but hadn't seen much of them since they headed for the bush a few years back. If nothing else, it would be good to be in touch again.

"Yo!" Frenchie's voice is unmistakable.

"Hi, kiddo. It's David McLure."

"David! Good, you got the message. I've been trying to get hold of you. I hear you're renting your second floor."

"Yeah, you interested?"

"Sure thing. Me, and the rest of the gals, of course. Hoo Hoo and Lucy are still up north winding up our farm life and I'm down here scoutin' for a new home. How much you chargin'?"

I tell her the rent.

She whistles. "That is truly a bargain, buddy. How can you do it?"

Performing Without a Net

"The place was a gift," I tell her. "All I need is enough to pay the taxes and keep it in decent shape."

"Well, it sounds great to me. We'll take it."

"Sight unseen?"

"I saw it years ago. It can't have changed too much. When can we move in?"

"Anytime. And, remember, it is more or less furnished."

"Suits us fine. This is wonderful, David. We have a lot of catching up to do. I better call the girls now," she says, preparing to hang up. "Oh, by the way, was that Zero who answered before?"

"Yeah."

"He sounded like shit. I didn't recognize his voice. Is he not feeling well?"

I give her a quick sketch of our health situation.

"Shit, David, I'm so sorry." She's silent a moment. "Anyway, tell him hi. We'll see you guys in the next couple of days, okay?"

"That's super, Frenchie. I'm looking forward to this."

I go shake Zero awake. "We should go eat, hon."

He's off somewhere. It takes him a moment to get back. He nods.

I call ahead to Bersani's with our order. When we've settled at our table, he smiles ruefully. "My mom called today when you were out. She's coming up again."

"Oh, lord," I groan. "She's not staying with us, is she?"

"Absolutely not!" he declares. "No, she'll be at the Sutton Place. She's going to drive me crazy soon enough without having her in our home."

"She was just here," I complain.

"Well, not really. It was last month when I was in the hospital."

"Seems like only yesterday to me," I reply, "but she is your mother, and she does seem concerned."

21

LABOUR OF LOVE

"I think the term is 'obsessed.' I just wish she wouldn't treat me like I'm already gone. I may have to strangle her."

"When's she coming? And for how long? How'd she feel about us living together again?" This information is important to me.

"It reassures her in some ways, I think. You know, better the devil she knows, than the one she doesn't. She'll never like the reality that you don't let her push you around."

Years ago when Zero first took me home to exhibit me to the folks in Arkansas, his mother, Edie, had been very hostile to both of us. On our first night, with a full cast of relatives assembled, she'd attacked and humiliated Zero until he was in tears. The relatives looked on with relish as though this was their favorite Friday evening blood sport. Finally, I stood up and called a halt to the proceedings. I tried to be polite, but when that proved futile, I'd been driven to curse her to everlasting suffering and sorrow in this world and the next.

The rest of the trip was spent in relative peace. The other kinfolk seemed quite relieved that someone had finally tackled Edie in a fair fight. She was a grim and hostile figure, staring balefully at Zero and me from the sidelines of every family event till we headed back to Canada.

I'd committed the unforgivable sin. I tangled with a Southern belle. And in her own home, no less. When we left, after two weeks of travel and family gatherings throughout the South, she didn't speak to me again for eight years. The situation, though often awkward, suited me just fine.

Zero seemed to have come to some reasonable accommodation with her over those years. I just stayed out of it. I didn't need her in my life any more, I'm sure, than she needed me. Their relationship consisted of infrequent phone calls and even less frequent visits.

A few years ago, after I nearly died with pneumocistis carini pneumonia, before Zero had moved out for his five-month dalliance with Clay, she's surprised me with a Christmas present and a note asking if we could start over again. I was touched. It felt good to have seemingly moved beyond the hostilities.

She became extremely hospitable. We visited back and forth. Zero and I would visit Arkansas and Texas for various family events. She and Sparky, her married lover, would come up here to wine and dine us at the best restaurants in town.

The most memorable, and recent, visit to the South was the gala celebration of Zero's sister's thirtieth birthday, which had degenerated into what the Little Rock newspapers still refer to as the "MacNoo Family Capital Hotel Shoot-Out." Sparky's wife had appeared at the event armed, intoxicated, and bent on bloody revenge. Shots were fired. Edie took a twenty-five-foot header off the hotel mezzanine into a large, lobster-shaped butter sculpture and Sparky barely escaped with his tenderest parts after Hilda tried to shoot them off.

Edie became almost sincere in her concern when Zero moved out to live with Clay, but I think, in her heart of hearts, she realized that he and I were for keeps, regardless of who else might be in our lives, or in our heads. You'd think she could understand that, with all the relationships she had up in the air at any given moment. But the concept of an enduring love in Zero's life always kept her slightly sour. And she never did get to know Jeff, so had no sense of that burst of sweet passion in Zero's life.

At any rate, although we had made some sort of peace, mostly I endured her, and she, me. Zero welcomed the end of the cold war, but cautioned me never to trust her. Although occasionally charming, she remains self-centered, mean-spirited, and obsessed with appearances. I never really became a fan.

"I told her she could only stay a few days," he assures me, "and that she wasn't to come till after Lesbian and Gay Pride Day."

"Sounds fair. Let's eat."

* * *

LABOUR OF LOVE

Snookums is in the kitchen talking to Zero when I come in from shopping.

"Precious, are you up to churning out a column for this issue of *City Magazine?*" he inquires.

"I'm not sure, but I'd like to try. Is that okay?"

"Of course it is," Snookums reassures him.

I put on water for tea. "You seem real perky this morning, Snooks."

"Oh, he's been seeing that Blaine boy who helped us move my stuff."

"That cute tall guy from Woody's?" I ask.

"Yes, darling." Snookums is blissful. "He seems to find me exotic. And I find him stimulating and possessed of, shall I say, rather substantial charms." He coughs daintily. "Unfortunately, the dear boy keeps six cats in his apartment. There is cat hair absolutely everywhere. I constantly feel as though I'm about to cough up a fur ball."

"Sounds gross," I say pouring the tea. "You should be rendez-vousing at your place."

"That's the plan, man!" He gets up and picks up Lance's photo from the mantel in the next room. "What's happening with you and this remarkably beautiful young man, David? I understood that he was your big new love."

"He is, but since Immigration tracked him down and sent him home, we've been trying to work something out. He's finishing his degree at Tulane in New Orleans. We talk every two or three days. It's not easy sustaining long-distance love," I lament.

"Precious, it's not easy sustaining love anywhere."

"I think that David's just fatigued by his situation," Zero pipes up. "Who would've thought that in one lifetime he'd fall head over heels for not one Arkansan, but two, and two from the same family?"

"Lance's some sort of cousin of Zero's," I explain. Lance's mother, Helen, is the product of a long-term relationship between

24

Performing Without a Net

Zero's grandfather, Walter Jackson MacNoo, and his housekeeper, Stellrita.

"I find it quite overwhelming," adds Zero. "I feel like I'm part of a romantic relay race."

"Oh, come on Zero," I say. "You know, I know, and Lance knows that you're my priority. I may love you both but I've loved you a lot longer."

"I know that, babe." He blows me a kiss. "Besides, it wouldn't be you if you didn't want to have your cake and eat it, too."

"Maybe you could all take some lessons from the Bermuda Triangle," Snookums says. "I hear they're moving in upstairs. That should be very interesting." He gives his turban a twist, gathers his papers, and actually skips down the front steps. He stops at the bottom to cough.

"You get that checked out, mister," I caution.

He rolls his eyes. "Fur balls!"

I've been taking the new drug for four days and it's working. For the first time in months the diarrhea is under control. I feel some energy returning. I have some appetite. Respite. I dare to hope.

Zero is struggling. Daily high fevers. Headaches. A new CAT scan reveals yet another lesion on his brain. Yet everyday he writes on, intent on somehow finishing the new book. We are into the final process of revisions. I read and edit. He rewrites. Snookums reads. We discuss. Zero continues to clean and tighten the work.

Finally, one morning he hands me the manuscript. "Can you get some copies made of this? It's done. It's ready to be sent out."

"Zero, that's amazing!" I take him in my arms. He's so frail, and again his body is burning. The completion of this book's been an act of pure will. I hold him for a long moment, then he pushes away from me.

25

LABOUR OF LOVE

"Sorry, David, but I've got to lie down. I've left some stamped envelopes out so can you mail it for me too, okay?"

"No problem, sweetheart."

"You are an angel."

"I'll be back shortly, as soon as I have this in the mail. Your present publishers have what—a thirty-day option?"

"Yes, we should hear by the end of July if they want it."

"They'll want it," I assure him.

He's stretched out on the couch asleep before I'm out the door.

Church Street is buzzing with anticipation of Lesbian and Gay Pride Day this weekend. Already the monster rainbow flag billows down the front of the 519 Community Centre. It's a bright, hot day. Cawthra Beach is full of parboiled boys flaunting their flesh in the sun. Seeing and being seen.

I used to love to be in the sun, but a couple of years on AZT has made me extremely photosensitive. Also, if the truth be known, my vanity precludes me exposing all these ribs to the general public.

I make the manuscript copies, do the mailing, and circle by the florist on Yonge Street. I buy three dozen yellow roses. I stop at the liquor store and buy a bottle of Veuve Cliquot. By the time I walk up the stairs at home, I'm exhausted.

Zero is sitting up looking tired as well, but also very satisfied with himself. On the table there is another bottle of Veuve Cliquot and an armload of yellow tulips. I set down my champagne and roses. We both laugh. "Happy anniversary!" I take his face in my hands and kiss him. He stands up unsteadily and presses himself against me. I'm amazed at how thin he's become. How thin we've both become.

"Twelve long years, David," he says.

"Through thick and thin."

"For richer, for poorer, in sickness and in health," he recites.

Performing Without a Net

"Til' death do us part?" I ask.

"I'm not sure even that will work." He laughs.

"Congratulations on the book. I'm so proud of you."

"We still have to see if they like it."

"Trust me. By the way, how did you get the tulips and champagne?"

"Oh, Searcy dropped by and I sent him on errands. His final court date and his nomination meeting are coming up and he's in a major flap."

"Mostly about what to wear, I bet."

"He's going to drop by later, before we go out to dinner."

"We're going out to dinner?"

"Yes, I think I'm feeling up to it. I made reservations at La Mexicana on Carlton. Sound okay?"

"Sounds great."

I put the champagne in the fridge and set some glasses in to chill. I arrange the flowers. They're glorious. The garden I've built in the back is a riot of bloom. The bright sunshine, the flowers inside and out. It's a good day.

Suddenly, I am very tired. "I need to lie down before all this social stuff happens," I confess.

"Me too."

I help him up from where he's sitting. We stretch out in the back bedroom. He's quickly asleep, head against my shoulder.

Twelve years. And what a time we've had.

I am deep in dreams when I hear Searcy yodeling at the door. "Yoo hoo! Darlings!"

I wander out, half-asleep, and open the door.

LABOUR OF LOVE

"It's such a drag being a local superhero. I can't even find a phone booth big enough to change my tights in anymore. Do you think they're making them smaller?" he exclaims, barely stopping for breath. "I tell you, David, with my court appearance on Friday, and my nomination, we hope, next week, and Pride Day on Sunday, I am in an absolute lather."

"You must be pretty confident about everything. Millie certainly seems to have your nomination campaign well in hand."

"Oh, Millie is as happy as a pig in shit. Like you said, she loves political organizing. I really do think I've got the nomination. Some of the New Democrat establishment aren't so happy with that prospect. They're not comfortable with me at all. I dare say, I'm just a tad too flamboyant for them."

"Oh, they've just got their assholes screwed on too tight. They'll calm right down once they realize you're about to win the election for them in November."

"I know. It's really my court appearance I'm worried about," he confesses. "We've done all the preliminary stuff. The judge gives her verdict at ten, Friday morning."

"I'll be there."

"Only if you're up to it," he cautions. "There will be lots of folks, including my loyal Queer Nation gang. I'm really not worried about enough support being there. I do worry about what to wear and I worry most about the judge."

"Just wear what you were attacked in," I advise. "That should be convincing."

"Well, probably," he admits, "but there are those jealous and unkind souls around who'd maintain that I should've been attacked a long time ago for wearing all that purple brocade."

"And what about the judge?"

"It's our old buddy, Uganda Dishwater's aunt. You know, Madame Justice Medusa Vanderplaats. Very, very scary!"

Performing Without a Net

Uganda had shown up at several parties over the years with this grim old auntie in tow. She was known, in our circle, as "The Conversation Killer." She would circulate through the crowd making what she thought was cocktail chatter. She'd fix her victim with her steely gaze, give her hand a perfunctory pump, squeak out a chilly smile and intone, "I am Madame Justice Medusa Vanderplaats, Supreme Court of Ontario. You may call me Medusa." She invariably left her conversation partner in a paralyzed state of terror like a rabbit frozen in the glare of headlights. Our longest chat had involved her informing me that she considered deep reflection to be a detriment to the efficient administration of the law and that she, therefore, tried to avoid it.

"It'll be fine. You might want to rethink the purple brocade, just in case she's wearing hers."

"Smart thinking, sister," he says, putting another bottle of champagne into the fridge. "If she did wear her brocade, we could go out for lunch afterward, like Edie and Doll in those hilarious mother and daughter getups they do."

"Edie prefers to think of them as sister outfits," I say sternly.

Searcy guffaws. "Of course, how could I have forgotten!" He takes a chilled bottle of bubbly and the glasses from the fridge. "Go give Zero a shake. I see Snookums coming down the street."

He wakens immediately. "Are they here?"

I give him my hand to help him up. Even his hands are burning. He walks unsteadily to the bathroom and splashes water on his face. I wait for him.

"Kind of shaky," he says, with a forced smile.

By the time we make it to the living room, Snookums is ensconced on the couch and the champagne has been poured.

Zero hails them, "Girlfriends!"

Both Snookums and Searcy rise and curtsey.

LABOUR OF LOVE

Snookums passes out the champagne. "I shouldn't be drinking this, but it is a special occasion. I am a reformed alcoholic, as you well know.

"Now, I want to make a toast to two wonderful men and a legendary, or should I say, notorious, relationship. You've had wonderful, independent lives, but have also been very special together. It's always been a pleasure to know Zero, and to know David, and to know Zero and David. Twelve years is a long time for any couple to be together, but, in gay years, it's a lifetime. I wish you many more."

"Hear! Hear!" booms Searcy. "You're fabulous, honeys. You don't have to pretend!"

Zero and I are both moved by Snookums's testimonial. We raise our glasses to them. "To our good friends," we say in unison, as though we had rehearsed it. We laugh.

Zero is suddenly animated. "We've hardly made a dent in this champagne," he proclaims. "There's another bottle in the fridge."

"Three, actually," says Searcy. "Snookums and I both brought extra."

"Just in case," adds Snookums.

"Well, why don't we see if Millie Gobert and the Bermuda Triangle are home," Zero suggests.

"I'll call 'em," I say.

Millie is home. Millie's always home. She's lived here forever. I kind of inherited her with the house. She adores Zero and me, although she's never understood the openness of the relationship. She was inconsolable the few months that Zero lived with Clay. She'd meet me on the stairs with the most forlorn look on her face, sighing and shaking her head mournfully. I took to slipping in and out of the back to avoid this performance. As soon as he returned, she perked right up again.

She's been retired for years. She was an ace trade union organizer. Now, she mostly drinks.

"Yes," she rasps over the phone. "I'll be down in a shake. I hope that big old Searcy's there. I have some final arrangements for his nomination I need to nail down with him."

I assure her that he's in the building, then hang up and phone the Bermuda Triangle. Hoo Hoo answers. She is very out of breath. "Oh, it's you, David," she pants.

"Were you in the middle of something?" I ask.

"Yes and no. We love that deep old tub up here, but none of us is as young, or as slender, as we once were. And when we're all in it at once you practically need a shoehorn to get in and out."

I can't imagine.

"Anyway, we were just finishing. What's up? The ceiling isn't leaking, is it?"

I assure her that our ceiling is fine and invite them down.

"Lovely," she enthuses. "I'll get these other gals dried off and we'll be down pronto."

"Well, they're all on the way," I announce.

Zero claps his hands. "Super!"

Millie arrives clutching her brandy, the drink of choice she swills by the tumblerful throughout the day.

"Hi, boys," she greets Snookums and Searcy. She gives Zero and me each a kiss on the cheek.

"Now, Searcy," she says, taking charge, "you come into the kitchen with me. I need to show you the final brochure for the nomination."

"Yes, boss." Searcy heaves himself to his feet and salutes. "But let's keep this brief. This is supposed to be a party."

"Yeah, yeah, yeah," she growls, "and your nomination is next week and I need to get this copy to the printer's. Come on, this will only take a minute."

* * *

31

LABOUR OF LOVE

The Bermuda Triangle come clattering down the stairs. They are all flushed and rosy, fresh from their bathtub frolics.

"Well, don't you look squeaky clean," I say.

"Clean as whistles," proclaims Lucy Culpepper.

"Love that tub," chimes in Frenchie.

"Champagne all around?" asks Snookums.

"You betcha!" Hoo Hoo goes to give him a hand.

"So here's to your anniversary, guys," says Lucy.

Searcy and Millie reappear. "What about my champagne?" she wails.

"Sorry, old girl," says Snookums, "I thought you were into the brandy."

"Of course, but I want some champagne to start," Millie replies.

Zero is quiet, but clearly enjoying having our old friends here. We've kept a low profile this past year with Jeff's spectacular passing and our own constantly changing health situations.

He gets up and puts some show tunes on the cassette player. He's very wobbly on his feet. Everyone pretends not to notice.

"What time is our reservation?" I ask.

"Seven-thirty," he replies. "This is nice here, though. Like old times. Would you mind terribly if we stayed in? We could order some of those great pizzas from Bersani's."

"Anything's fine with me, Zero."

"Do any of you have plans?" I ask. "Zero and I have decided to stay in and have pizza. We'd like you to join us."

Everyone is agreeable.

"Pizza and champagne!" exclaims Snookums. "You boys always were such a class act."

Lucy pours the third bottle of champagne. "When is your bashing verdict?" she asks Searcy.

"Friday morning at ten in Courtroom Twelve at Old City Hall. I hope you'll all be there."

"You bet," replies Lucy. "I hope they throw the book at them."

"Who's the judge?" inquires Frenchie.

"Uganda's aunt, Madame Justice Medusa Vanderplaats," Searcy replies, with a grimace. "For all I know, she may approve of gay bashing. She's such a joyless old thing."

"Oh, yes," interjects Hoo Hoo, "I've met her at some of Uganda's dinner parties through the years. Good luck."

"Then, of course, I'm one of the Grand Marshals for the Lesbian and Gay Pride Day parade on Sunday. And I'll be emceeing as well. Then on Tuesday my nomination for the municipal election happens, and by then I should be dead and you can bury me," announces Searcy.

"You shouldn't push too hard, Searcy," says Zero. "You're not invincible."

"Yes, I am," he replies.

Later, after they've gone, we sit out in the garden in the soft twilight. The honeybees which appear every evening are busy at their sweet tasks. The air is warm and spicy with the scent of the bed of nicotiana by the deck. Zero is in the new rocking chair I bought him to celebrate his move back home. I'm beside him, head against his knee. Dinah Washington croons on the CD player. We can hear the noise of Church Street as people hit the streets for the evening. Zero looks drained. He catches my eye. We smile.

"You know those wills we made when you first got sick?" he asks.

"I've never changed mine. You still get everything."

"Likewise." He squeezes my hand.

We had left everything to each other, but had a real dilemma about all the art and beautiful objects we had accumulated together over the years. We wanted them to go to good homes when we both were gone. So we labeled everything with specific instructions as to who was to get what. It was actually quite a hoot trying to match our collected artwork with our friends' personalities.

"I'm wasted, honey," he sighs. "Can we go in and curl up? I can barely keep my eyes open."

He's already in bed by the time I lock the doors and get the lights out. I slip my arms around him and curl myself tightly against his back. He's burning hot again. He opens his eyes and twists around to kiss me.

"Sweet dreams," I whisper.

I call Searcy early Friday morning. "Listen, Searcy, Zero has to go up to Sunnybrook for a CAT scan and he's pretty shaky. Can you do court without us?"

"Darlin', how dare you even ask that? Of course, I can do court without you. How are you doing yourself?" he inquires.

"A bit weak. This new drug seems to be working, but I have no appetite, so every pound I've lost is a major chore to try to put back on again.

"I wish that were my problem," he moans.

"Enjoy every ounce of it, Searcy. I'd sooner have perfectly explainable weight gain than unexplainable weight loss. You may need every bit of that fabulous flesh someday."

"I hear you," he says. "I hope they have air conditioning in that courtroom. This heat wave is hellish."

"They say it's going to last all month. That's scary. Thank goodness this house is so cool. Are you ready for this today, hon?"

"Yes, I think so. I may be tempted to heave a couple more of those greaseballs against the wall, but shall endeavor to maintain my goddesslike serenity in the face of any provocation. I am unclear just what will happen today."

"Well, I thought she was giving a verdict."

"I don't know. Last time the bashers' lawyer went on and on about how they were just defending themselves against the sexual advances of an obviously sex-crazed giant degenerate. Little *moi!* My lawyer just said that the facts of the case spoke for themselves. I would feel more confident if she had given those obvious facts a bit of a hand."

"How did old Medusa take all that?"

"With total, stony-faced silence. It was pretty ominous."

"Surely she wouldn't dismiss the charges?"

"Who knows? If she does, there will be hell to pay at Old City Hall. Lots of folks are going to be there, and people are really worked up about this."

"I hope it goes well. We'll be back from the hospital mid-afternoon. We'll be anxious for the news."

"Okay, doll. I need to run now, struggle into my outfit and fluff up the old hair a bit. We'll talk later. Thanks for calling."

The hospital visit is wearing for both of us. Zero is very quiet. He holds my arm tightly. Late in the afternoon we finally get a cab and head downtown. He hasn't said five words through the entire excursion.

"Did Dr. Fieldstone have any news?" I ask.

"Yes, the alternative therapy she's been trying doesn't seem to be working. There's another lesion." He speaks so softly and slowly I have to strain to hear him.

"Damn!" I exclaim.

"Yes, that's what I say, too. Damn!"

We hear the whistles and shouting when we turn on to Maitland from Jarvis. We get the cab to let us out at the Queen's Dairy. Snookums

35

and Frenchie spot us from across the street. His turban is a brilliant turquoise and Frenchie is wearing her horns.

These days, she often wears a yellow baseball cap with little stuffed moose horns stitched to the top. I guess they're part of her return to nature during the past few years in the bush. Spiritually, she apparently thinks she's a moose.

They scamper across the street to our corner. They are both talking breathlessly.

"You should have been there darlings!" enthuses Snookums. "*Quelle* performance!"

"By Searcy?" I ask.

"By everybody!" shouts Frenchie gleefully.

"So tell. Tell." Zero is suddenly energized.

"Well, the court was full," begins Snookums. "Even the hallway was jammed."

"Old Medusa asked for final statements. The bashers' lawyer repeated his shit from the preliminaries," adds Frenchie. "He also said his clients were considering laying attempted murder charges against Searcy for deliberately trying to give them AIDS. He asked for all charges against his clients to be dismissed. The room went crazy at that point and Medusa had to threaten to clear it. Then Searcy's lawyer, that dreamboat, Harriet Hamburg, made a brief statement, again saying that the facts spoke very clearly for themselves. She did ask if Searcy might address the court. Old Medusa mulled that over for a moment, looking very stern, but then over the kids' lawyer's objections, she said she would like to hear what Mr. Goldberg had to say."

"It was truly a great Goldberg moment," says Snookums. "When he rose to his feet the room went very quiet. He thanked the judge, then said that he had lived and worked in this city and in our community for most of his life. He told her how much he loves this town and his place in it. But, he told her, 'I have been insulted and attacked on the streets where I live. I, and many others, do not feel safe in this city that is our home. If the law is worth anything,' he continued, 'it must ensure that all of us can move with freedom and dignity and absolute safety anywhere in our town at any hour.' I can't do him justice, precious. He was so impassioned and he wasn't acting. He was crying when he sat down. And he wasn't alone.

"The kids, their families and friends, all seemed to think it was very funny. One of the boys snorted with laughter," Snookums continues. "But, Medusa froze him with a look, then after a long silence, she sat back and said, 'I agree completely with Mr. Goldberg. I find these young men contemptible and abhor the circumstances that allow and perpetuate their mindless and murderous homophobia. I find all five guilty as charged and sentence them each to four years imprisonment. I am disturbed by the apparent reluctance of the police to act to stem this violence and I find the sensational and inflammatory nature of the arguments made in defense of these hateful young men to be lamentable.'

" 'Your honor,' interjected the defense lawyer, 'this is disgraceful. There will be an appeal.'

" 'Your privilege, counselor,' snapped Medusa. 'Court is adjourned.' "

"Well, all hell broke loose," says Frenchie. "Our folks went crazy. Everybody was whooping and whistling. The bashers were outraged. Two of them were crying like babies. Their families were cursing and wailing. The kid who had laughed earlier leapt over the table shouting, 'You fucking whore!' Old Medusa was real cool. She picked up her papers, and very calmly ordered the bailiff to clear the court. The cops and court officials were milling around. They seemed quite confused by all the hubbub. Anyway, this kid is moving toward Medusa screaming, 'You sorry bitch! You fuckin', sorry old bitch!" And nobody was stopping him. It was a madhouse. Then Searcy caught up to the kid, grabbed him by the back of the neck and lifted him off the ground. With one hand! He shook the kid very, very hard. I was afraid he'd break his neck. The kid looked absolutely starkers with fright. One brush with an enraged Searcy Goldberg must be terrifying. Twice in one lifetime should just about do him. Then Searcy carried the kid, still with one hand, across the room, dropped him in front of the guards, and said, 'Get rid of this thing.'

"When the uproar finally settled down and we were filing out, Madame Justice said, 'Thank you very much, Mr. Goldberg.' "

"Searcy nodded, gave her a very elaborate curtsey, and sailed out," Snookums adds. "Then we had this spontaneous march down Queen to Yonge and back up here."

"Is Searcy there now?" Zero asks wearily.

"No. Actually someone from his defense committee is thanking the crowd. They've been at it awhile. He's at your place lying down. He's exhausted," Frenchie says.

"And so are we," I say.

"We'll walk you to the door. We should have done that right away. The last thing you need is to be standing out here in this heat, precious." Snookums squints at us anxiously in the still-bright evening sunshine.

The crowd is beginning to disperse, so there are lots of people who want to stop and talk. The four of us push on through. They say goodnight at the doorstep.

Searcy is sitting in the big armchair with his legs tucked under him. He's sipping tea. "What a day!" he exclaims. "I was beginning to worry about you two."

I tell him that Snookums and French have given us the news.

"I'm wiped out," says Searcy. "Thank goodness I have keys to your place. My tired old dogs were just about ready to lie down and die." He looks at us intently, then slowly gets to his feet. "I'll be off now. You guys both look completely bushed."

"Well, hon," I say, "I'm so glad court went well. Imagine Madame Justice Medusa Vanderplaats joining you in the pantheon of Queer Nation sainthood."

"Just imagine!" He laughs. "Now I'm going to soak this weary carcass in lovely bubbles for two or three hours. You two guys get some rest."

I'm up early. I want to water the garden while it's still relatively cool. The city crews are already delivering the barricades at the end of the block to redirect traffic for tomorrow's Pride Day celebrations. I check on Zero. He seems to be sleeping soundly. His forehead is cool.

I can hear the women upstairs beginning to stir. They seem to be chasing one another around. There is a great deal of shrieking and exuberant laughter.

I smile. I think they must keep Millie in a state of constant agitation.

I make coffee and sit down with the papers. The *Star* has a large shot of Searcy addressing supporters on the stairs of the courthouse. Great. There is a small editorial inside praising Madame Justice Vanderplaats's decision. The *Globe and Mail* has a discreet paragraph under local news. The *Sun* has an extreme close-up of Searcy on its cover. He looks like he was photographed through a fishbowl. The headline screams, DERANGED SOCIALIST DRAG QUEEN MAY BE CHARGED WITH DELIBERATELY SPREADING AIDS! I rip out the articles and tape the good photo to the fridge. I sharpen my pencil and sit down to my crossword.

Zero calls from the back, "Coffee on?"

"Yeah, you want it there, or are you getting up?"

"Getting up."

I walk back in time to give him my hand and help him to his feet.

"Hey, no fever!" He smiles. "It's been a while since that happened. Is that coffee as good as it smells?"

"Mm-hmm." I help him into his robe, then go back to pour his brew. We sit out in the back.

Despite his new fascination with gardening, he doesn't actually want to garden. But he is intrigued by the variety of plants and what I do with them. His interest is a real delight. I had a hunch this spring when he was in the hospital that this might be our last garden together. I wanted it to be spectacular. And it is.

"This is going to be a crazy week, David," he warns. "We both need to pace ourselves."

"Well, I'm working at the AIDS Action Now! table tomorrow and I'd like to march in the parade, if I'm up to it."

"I just know that I'm not. I'll wander around a bit, but I'd like for us to have dinner together. Okay? And let's not have people over this year."

"I'm with you on that. When does Edie arrive?"

"July Fourth. She still doesn't understand that it's not a holiday here." He shakes his head.

"I think she honestly does want to take care of you."

"Yes, for about fifteen minutes. I know she'd stick me in a hospice, or some nightmare institution in Arkansas, the moment things got messy." He's silent a moment. "Promise me, David, that if things go haywire and I'm the one who goes first, that you'll keep me here at home to the end, if you can possibly do it."

"I promise, Zero, but I bet if push comes to shove it could get quite messy with your mom."

"Yes, I know," he agrees. "But remember you have complete authority over all my affairs."

"Well, she has been sweeter these last couple of years."

"Yes, so she has, but don't ever trust her," he warns again. "With Edie, there's a string on everything, and a hook on every string."

I get up and refill our cups. "Any plans for today?"

"A couple of letters to type maybe, but I'm tired from yesterday. And, I'm not kidding about the holes in my brain. I get kind of confused. Disoriented," he says, shaking his head. "And you've seen my handwriting lately. I write stuff down, then I have no idea what I've written. My biggest nightmare is coming true.

"But you know," he continues, "all those times I said I'd end it if all this started to happen? I'm not so sure anymore. Moving back down here, finishing this new novel, the collection of columns coming out in the fall. Suddenly, so much good stuff is happening. Yes, it's late, but it's not too late. I just don't feel the kind of urgency and disappointment I was feeling before. It's hard to believe, huh? It feels like I'm reaching some sort of peace and rather than end it, I want to enjoy it."

"Well, thank goodness," I exclaim. "When you were in the hospital in April and were reading all that Hemlock Society stuff, you were so damned disagreeable. If you had stayed that miserable, it's likely someone would have killed you before you had a chance to do it yourself."

"I know, hon," he laughs. "The day I tried to brain you with that Louise Hay book was the worst. I was just so angry and afraid. Mostly about not being able to do enough in the time I had left. And, of course, there were Mom and Doll sitting bug-eyed and mournful at my bedside all day long."

"Maybe she won't stay so long this time," I say hopefully.

"Dream on! She's got an open ticket. What are you up to today?" he asks.

"I'll be around here. I have some garden work to do and some paperwork for the AIDS Network steering committee I need to finish for next week."

"Shit, David," he says with some irritation, "I wish you hadn't let yourself be elected as chair of that thing again. You know those organizations can continue without you. But you think you're so damned indispensable. It's like you have to keep in constant motion. Like some damned hummingbird."

"Well, who's the guy who just forced himself to finish a novel with two T cells, or was it three? Let's face it, baby, we're a great match. High-energy guys with lots of obsessions."

"You're right, but it's easier for me to tell you to stop, than to tell myself. Anyway, I want today to be a quiet one 'cause tomorrow will be a killer. They're expecting record-high temperatures and about a hundred thousand people."

"If you want," I suggest, "we could set a chair out for you right out there on the corner. You could hold court."

"No, I'll wander a bit, go to the AIDS Memorial, check out some booths, check out some boys. I'll try to meet you somewhere during the march, if I'm still on my feet."

"Good," I say, "I'll be the blond one."

He grins.

"I'll go to the AIDS Memorial first thing before it gets crowded, then do my AIDS Action Now! stint and, hopefully, I'll still have the energy left to march," I continue. "Quite frankly, I can't imagine not marching."

"I know, I kind of feel the same way."

I get up and start repotting some begonias. He watches, occasionally asking questions. After a while he just lies there in the morning sun. Head thrown back. Asleep.

Sunday morning I get up early. I shrug into my AIDS Action Now! tank top and my jeans. I automatically reach down and brush Zero's forehead. He's very hot. Shit!

I make coffee, then go to the garden and cut two roses, a yellow one and a white one. I leave him the yellow bloom. I write a note— "Happy Pride Day, Little Flower. Coffee's made. See you in a while. I love you." I sign it "Hummingbird."

* * *

Performing Without a Net

Church Street is already teeming with people. Everyone is trying to do their last-minute preparations while there is still some cool morning air.

I stop to talk to the Bermuda Triangle and some of their friends on the steps of the Second Cup. They've already set up the Women's Common table and are now just looking for trouble. Frenchie and Lucy Culpepper keep up a constant banter about what they call "hot babes" passing by. Hoo Hoo looks bored and disgusted with all this, but she doesn't fool me for a moment. She has a wicked reputation as a lesbian Lothario much less given to talk than to direct action. She catches my eye and gives me a sly smile. She knows that I'm on to her. We've known each other a long, long time, from back when we were organizing lesbians and gay men on the Prairies in the early seventies. We're exactly the same age, too, which has always led us to claim a special bond. Hoo Hoo and I have few secrets.

"Is the rose for Little David?" she asks. I nod.

The kid I had been involved with, back when I met Hoo Hoo, had the bad luck to be called David as well. Since he was much younger than I and less well known, everyone called him "Little David." He and I both hated that, but what can you do? The tyranny of nicknames!

Anyway, Little David and I broke up in 1977, though we managed to stay close. I was his first. The first man he had ever kissed, the first man he'd ever danced with, the first man he'd ever made love with, the first man he'd ever loved. And I adored him. We grew apart, but did manage to keep in touch through the years.

He was diagnosed with AIDS several years ago, and died in the fall of 1988, while I was in the hospital battling my first round of PCP. Of course, I never had a chance to say good-bye. This will be the third year I've left him a rose on the Pride Day AIDS Memorial.

Hoo Hoo squeezes my elbow. "See you in a while, love."

43

LABOUR OF LOVE

Lucy stops her catcalling for a moment. "We'll all keep an eye out for Zero, David. He hasn't looked too steady lately."

"Thanks, Luce."

As I turn to leave, Frenchie pinches my butt. "Nice ass, buster," she growls. "Pity you're not a dyke."

"Can't have everything," I respond. We all laugh.

At Cawthra Park, I'm one of the first at the Memorial. As always, there are new names. Surprises. People you thought, or hoped, were just out of town. The acceleration of names, of numbers, is dizzying. Where will mine be? In this year's tally? Or next? How many of my friends will be here before and after me? How much more of my history, our history, will be torn away, replaced by a memorial plaque and some ephemeral memories? And so many of the holders of even those memories are going or gone. Somehow we have to record these losses and celebrate these lives. We need to keep on living the life and telling the tales. For ourselves. We have to keep this community alive. Because nobody else will.

I find Little David and tuck the white rose by his name. I stay a moment. Then it's time to go.

The AIDS Action Now! display is on the other side of the park. I help set up, but it's already hot and I'm flagging. I hand out brochures for a couple of hours. The crowd is massive. There is a great deal of hugging and greeting to do. I'm on the lookout for Zero. Afraid for him in the press of urgent bodies. As my shift ends, I spot him across the park. I try to catch him. He looks very pale and intense. He's too far ahead of me and I lose sight of him. After a couple of frustrating and futile searches through the park, I head over to where the march is assembling.

Performing Without a Net

* * *

My view of the main performance stage is blocked by a gaggle of tall boys, but I can hear Searcy finishing his spiel as master of ceremonies. He exhorts everyone to come out of their closets, the bars, the beer gardens, their air-conditioned apartments and into the streets to join us.

"Today, the City of Toronto is ours!" he proclaims to a riot of whistles and applause.

Searcy descends from the stage. The crowd parts. He's all dolled up in a sort of twisted, Little Bo Peep–fantasy number. Like some gargantuan, deranged poppet, with lots of ribbons and flounces, and acres of frilly underwear. A spectacular Grand Marshal for the day. And won't he be resplendent on the City Council as well, I muse. I giggle out loud at the prospect.

He spots me and barges over. He lifts me off the ground in a giant bear hug. "Happy Pride Day, David!" he shouts. "You look positively butch in those tight, little jeans and that *Action Equals Life* T-shirt."

"Searcy," I point out, "I think the term is emaciated, not butch."

"Get over it, girl!" he exclaims. "You're too sensitive. All those boys I see checking you out are not measuring you for a coffin. They just think you're hot. The only interest they have in your bones, hon, is in jumpin' 'em. So smarten up." He puts me down. Lecture over.

"Where's Zero?"

"I'm trying to find him," I reply.

"I worry about him in this heat, and in this crowd," he says. "I'll keep an eye out for him."

The Grand Marshals' pink convertible is ready. The jolly, red-faced lesbian sharing the honor is already aboard in her leather tux. She must be melting. She gives Searcy a big kiss and a hand up to the backseat.

LABOUR OF LOVE

The car begins to move slowly. The Grand Marshals wave, blow kisses, and toss condoms. The AIDS Action Now! contingent is close behind. I scoot underneath our banner and find Lucy Culpepper. For years we've taken advantage of marches and demonstrations to walk together and catch up with what's happening in our lives. I'm distracted today, scanning the huge crowd for Zero.

Snookums, in a hot-pink Pride Day turban, darts out from the sidewalk by Maple Leaf Gardens to join us. There are hugs and kisses all round. He is soon off loping along beside the Grand Marshals' car, ostensibly to chat with Searcy, but mostly because the lithe and lovely Blaine is at the wheel.

Snookums returns all atwitter, because Blaine has asked him to go to a hot-tub party in Cabbagetown later.

"What if my turban were to unwind?" he wails.

"Surely Blaine has seen your naked head by now," I say.

"Yes, yes, of course, and it drives him wild." He shakes his head. "Can you believe it!?"

"Then, if he loves your bald knob, don't worry about it," Lucy counsels.

"I'm not worried about dear Blaine, precious," he replies. "It's those other thoughtless, guppy youths who will be there, undoubtedly eager to snicker at the imperfections of others."

"Well, Snookums," I chime in, "it might be the moment to bite the bullet and go *au naturel*. You've obviously captivated Blaine, so why not say to hell with the rest?"

"We'll see, precious," he pats his turban protectively. "You could be right."

* * *

Performing Without a Net

At the corner of Bloor and Church, a lesbian giantess named Tucker, clad only in jockey shorts, dances atop a phone booth. She's in the same spot every year. I stop to watch her gyrations.

I'm exhausted, and I still haven't spotted Zero. Then I see him. He's about a quarter of a block south and leans with one hand against a hydro pole. I unhook my arms from Lucy's and head for him. He looks up and sees me. He leaves the sidewalk and starts toward me. His steps are short and jerky.

"I knew I'd find you," he declares, short of breath.

"I've been looking for you," I say. I hold him hard. I am crying. So is he.

We sway together in the street. "Let's finish this parade," he whispers.

"Are you up for this?" I ask.

"Yes, but let's take it real slow."

Lucy moves in to take his other arm. Snookums frolics up to embrace him and wish him the best of the day. Assured that the situation is now under control, he dodges ahead through the milling crowd to make his arrangements with Blaine.

The rest of the parade passes us by, till there's just the three of us walking slowly, arm in arm, down the middle of Church Street. Lucy walks us to our door, then heads upstairs for a hot soak before she hits the streets again.

"I was feeling panicky out there," he confesses. He's stretched out on the couch. "I couldn't make my feet work."

"I could see that," I say.

"Fucking toxo! What am I going to do?" He shades his eyes with one hand, and massages the side of his head where the lesions are sited with the other. "Can you come and lie down with me here? But please bring me some water. I feel dehydrated."

"Sure thing, darlin'," I reply.

47

LABOUR OF LOVE

He shifts over to make room beside him. It's noisy outside. Wild music. Crazy laughter and shouting. We are asleep in moments.

It's dark when he shakes me awake. You can still hear the festivities winding down in the street. "Hungry?" he whispers.

"I could eat," I reply.

"Let's go to The 457. I want a big ol' steak," he announces.

I help him up, and we're out the house in moments. As we cross to the other side of Maitland, his knees buckle. I can hardly hold him up. He gives me a little smile and shrugs. "What can I do?" he asks.

We walk through the crowded bar at The 457 to the odd little restaurant hidden in the back. Dinner back here is a Pride Day tradition for us. Usually we're with an exuberant gang of friends, fresh from the day's celebrations. Excited, tired, horny, and ravenous. Tonight, though, the place is strangely empty. The usually cheerful Yugoslavs who run the place are glum. Their homeland is beginning to unravel. The waiter has not heard from his parents in a month. We pick at our food. Our appetites have disappeared.

The walk home is a trial. His legs seem unable to respond. At home I help him undress, then I make us tea. Put out all but the bedside lamps, and unplug the phones. I slip between the covers. He's already asleep.

Pride Day. Right now, I don't feel particularly proud. Right now, I feel sad and exhausted. Right now, I feel afraid.

The phone rings at six o'clock. Shit! I thought I'd unplugged them all so we both could sleep in. It's Zero's mom, Edie.

"Well, hi y'all!" she says. "How y'all doing? Put that lazy boy of mine on the phone, will ya. I want to give him all of my flight details."

"Edie," I protest, "it's very early in the morning here and he's fast asleep. He's really worn out. Can I write down your details or could he call you back?"

She gives a loud, exasperated sigh. "Well, I guess so, but I just know he'd want to talk to me."

My efforts not to wake Zero have failed. He sits up in a rage. His hair is frightening. He looks like the wrath of God.

"Who the hell is that?" he snarls.

"Your mother," I say timidly, anxious not to cross him in his agitated state.

"Give me that damned thing!" he roars. "Mom, is this an emergency?" he demands. "I don't care. I need my sleep. You know that unless it's a real dire emergency, you are not to call here at odd times, like the crack of dawn. Now get a grip! And stop whimpering," he berates her. "It will be easier for me to call your airline for details rather than have you call at this hour with information that you've probably written down incorrectly in the first place." He slams the phone down.

"What is she on?" he says, tiredly, burying his head in his hands.

"Surely she's not drunk at this hour?" I ask. For years, I used to recognize her calls before she'd even speak. I'd hear the telltale rattling of the ice cubes in her ever-present tumbler of scotch, and just hand the phone to Zero.

She's been very ill recently with both her liver and pancreas in full revolt. Theoretically, she's off the sauce. She prefers not to talk about her alcohol-related diseases. Rather, she tells people that she has put aside drink, so she can be strong for Zero in these troubled times.

"She's probably on some sort of pharmaceutical cocktail," I venture, anxious to calm him down.

"Who cares?" he mutters. "She should have the common courtesy to be passed out at this hour and not harassing exhausted sick people." He's getting himself worked up again. "She's taking a limo in from the airport, so we hardly need her arrival details," he continues to gripe.

LABOUR OF LOVE

"I'll never get back to sleep," he complains, flopping back down. He's asleep as his head hits the pillow. I can feel the heat from his fever. It's alarming.

There will be no more sleep for me now. I lie beside him wondering how we'll survive the next few days. The prospect is daunting.

I toss and turn trying to find the path back to sleep, but the way eludes me. I get up and go out to the garden. There's been a light rain during the night and all the growing things sparkle. I pull a chair over beneath the Siberian olive and lie back. The new sun falls directly on my face. Bliss.

"Happy Canada Day!" exclaims Snookums, appearing with Blaine at the side of the house. They're holding hands. "I knew you'd be back here, precious."

He's swapped his Pride Day pink for a turban fashioned from the Canadian flag. Blaine is clad only in pale blue boxer shorts and dirty, pink high-top running shoes.

"How was the hot-tub party?" I inquire.

"Hot!" Snookums cries enthusiastically.

Blaine smiles dreamily. "We're just on the way home," he says, running his hand up and down Snookums's back. "We just thought we'd see if the coffee was on."

Snookums beams.

"Sure. But I'm too lazy to move. You know where it is. Help yourselves."

Blaine turns to go inside. It looks like someone has taken a bite out of his boxers, and the smooth whiteness of his butt flirts tantalizingly through.

"Mmmmm. Delicious!" I exclaim softly.

Snookums is delirious. "You cannot imagine," he says, his eyes rolling back in his head. "Who would have ever believed this, at my advanced age?"

"Your age? You're not that old, Snooks."

"Well, no, but I am as bald as a billiard ball," he protests.

"Give it a rest, Snookums. You're a handsome guy. A lot more people are attracted to you than you ever seem to think."

"Sure, and that's easy for you to say, Mister Famous Gay Activist."

Blaine returns with coffee for them and a refill for me. He's singing Travis Tritt's "Here's a Quarter. Go Call Someone Who Cares." He has an oddly sexy, off-key voice. He stretches out on the deck, with his head pillowed in Snookums's lap. "I am totally fucked out," he murmurs, closing his eyes. Snookums strokes the short brush-cut nestled between his thighs. He smiles distractedly.

I leave the two of them to their sex-soaked reverie and slip into the house to check on Zero. He's kicked off all the covers. He's very hot to the touch. He opens his eyes for a moment. "David, where are we?" he asks, in a panic.

"At home, hon," I assure him, brushing his hair back from his sweating brow.

"Oh good," he sighs, and slips back into sleep immediately.

I pull the sheet up over him and refill the water glass by the bed.

I curse his doctors. Six months of throbbing headaches, constant fevers and chills, and although there was obviously something happening in his head, not one of them thought to give him a CAT scan. Then, finally, just before Christmas last year, they got around to checking on the obvious. Toxoplasmosis! Two lesions on the left-hand side of his brain. Then, of course, they threw all this debilitating treatment at him. And now he seems to just get sicker and sicker. Nothing seems to work. I begin to think the bastards just left it too long. I am frustrated and furious. Although I try to avoid thinking about it, more and more I'm afraid I'm going to lose him.

LABOUR OF LOVE

He, of course, has been working too hard. Promoting the new book, pushing to finish the sequel. Desperate. Driven. Afraid now that he's going to run out of time.

He'd ended up in the hospital in April. We both did. Dr. Fieldstone insisted we be placed in the same room. We thought it was mighty sweet of her. You know, the family that rehydrates together . . . That got old, though, in a big hurry. We got on each other's nerves. Fast. Having Edie and Doll here hadn't helped. It feels now like history is about to repeat itself. I don't want it to. I just want this all to stop. I kiss his burning forehead.

"How is he?" whispers Snookums from the doorway.

"Feverish again."

"He's got me worried sick, precious. You know you can call me for anything, at any time, if you need me."

"I know, and I will."

"I wanted to say bye 'cause we're going to my place now to collapse," he says, stifling a small yawn. "Blaine has a shift at Woody's this evening, then we're going down to Harbourfront to catch the Canada Day fireworks. If you need me just leave me a message. I'll also check with you before we head out."

"Thanks, hon. I think we'll probably stick close to home. We want to be at Searcy's nomination tomorrow, and Edie arrives on the Fourth of July."

He chuckles. "Now that's scary. You better take it easy, David. I worry about you, too."

As they disappear around the corner of the house, Blaine gives me a saucy, sleepy grin and blows me a lazy kiss.

I hear the phone ringing. I rush to get it before it wakens Zero. "Hi," I say, a bit out of breath.

"David? What's happening, sweet thing? You sound winded."

Performing Without a Net

"Oh, Lance," I exclaim, "how good to hear your voice."

"How's our Zero?"

"Not so great. Lots of fevers. A bit confused."

"Shit! What have we done to deserve this? And you, my darling, is that new drug still working?"

"Seems to be. At least, I've stopped losing weight. Haven't gained any, though."

"Wish I was there to fatten you up."

"I wish you were, too."

"God, I miss you, David. Being apart is so hard. Especially when y'all need all the lovin' you can get. Do you want me to come up? I can pick up this semester another time."

"No, babe," I say firmly, "you need to be there and we can't afford to fuck up with Immigration again."

Lance and I'd met and fallen in love in Little Rock on the weekend of Doll's gala thirtieth birthday party. He'd come for a two-week visit last spring. That visit was extended and extended. He'd finally found an under-the-table job at a local bar. But, after two months, someone reported him to Immigration and he'd been ordered to leave the country at once. The whole circumstance was nightmarish. Zero and I had lived through virtually the same scenario years ago. Too many star-crossed romances with beautiful boys from Arkansas could make a person crazy. And maybe it has.

The relationship with Zero is so rich and deep, so much a part of me. This thing with Lance, though, is hot and new. Fresh passion, with sizzling sex, like I haven't had since my earliest days with Zero. Before he got bored with me in bed. Before he got bored with himself.

Having the two of them crowded into my life is a dilemma. I, however, am not about to choose. I've made it clear to both that that's how it is. Zero's my priority, though, because he needs me most. Also I've loved Zero the longest and Lance understands that. Or he says that he does.

LABOUR OF LOVE

"Lance, you know we've agreed you are to stay until you finish Tulane in the fall," I lecture him. "We'll figure out then how to get you here permanently. We'll work it out somehow."

"Maybe you could adopt me," he suggests. "I'd love to be fucking my daddy. Is there a law about that?"

"I don't know, you're the law student. But it seems like a great idea, sonny." I laugh. "I do wish I could sponsor you. It would sure make life easier. Are things all right there?"

"Boring," he groans. "I don't know much, because I don't get out much. I'm headed for Little Rock, July Fourth, so there should be fresh news. I'll give you a call from there on Saturday. Okay?"

"Sure. Edie arrives here on the Fourth, so I'll be desperate for a sane voice by then."

"I can't guarantee that." He chuckles.

"Give my love to your mom and Stellrita."

"You betcha."

"Does Stellrita know how ill Zero is?" I ask.

"I think so. It's hard to pin down what she knows, or doesn't know, on any given day. Edie has declared war on my grandmother again," he reports.

"What about this time? You'd think she'd realize that she can't win, when she mixes it up with Stellrita. What happened?"

"Well, Grandmother had rabies," he begins.

"Rabies!" I exclaim. "How in hell did she get rabies? Is she alive? What's going on, Lance?"

"Cool it, lover, she's all right. You know they'd need the A-bomb to take her out. She was mighty sick, though."

"I know. It's a horrible disease, often fatal, and apparently the cure is nearly as bad as the disease. A friend of mine was bitten by a bat, just before our high-school grad. He didn't get treated in time. He went into a coma and died within a couple of days. How in hell did Stellrita get rabies?"

"Well, apparently, she was bitten by what she calls a 'varmint,' probably a rabid squirrel. She didn't tell anyone. Just slapped some of that miracle mud she insists on covering herself with on the bite. Mom says she was actin' a bit stranger than usual.

"Next thing Mom knew, Grandmother was staggering down the street, foaming at the mouth. She went over to where Edie has her semiretirement job, buffing her nails and answering the occasional phone call. Everyone else was on their lunch break. Grandmother burst in raving and announced, 'Edie, I have contracted me a case of the hydrophobia.' She had seen *Old Yeller*, I guess, because she had it in her head that they shoot you if you're infected. She told Edie, that if the pest control authorities were going to hunt her down, she'd decided to take someone with her. Said she'd got to thinking about who among her many acquaintances deserved rabies as much as she did. Apparently that was difficult, since so many qualified, but she informed Edie that her name just kept coming up. And since Edie's office was within a reasonable staggering distance from Stellrita's porch, she had decided to get on over and, as she so sweetly put it, 'Bite your evil butt, devil woman!'

"Edie went berserk. She tried to make a break for it, but Stellrita blocked her escape, growling and foaming. She chased Edie halfheartedly around the room a couple of times, then suddenly went rigid and fell over right there in a coma. Edie fled screaming out into the street.

"Her coworkers came back from lunch, found Stellrita, and called an ambulance. At the hospital, she rallied for a moment and told them she didn't need a doctor, she needed a vet. Then she slipped back into her coma. By any reasonable medical prognosis, she shouldn't have survived. She lay there for five days. When they checked her on the morning of the sixth, she was gone. They found her back on her porch. She pulled her gun. Wouldn't let them touch her.

"The public health authorities just said, let her be. Grandmother says it was a fascinating, new experience. Rare, indeed, after a hundred twenty-odd years. Quite frankly, I'm not at all convinced that she didn't stage the whole thing."

LABOUR OF LOVE

"I don't suppose it would be very healthy to suggest that," I say. "And what about poor Edie? She hasn't breathed a word about this to us."

"Well, Mom says she seems okay. She may be a bit unstrung by it all, but it's always a little hard to tell. And the *Gazette* did feature a wild shot of her having an absolute hissy fit in the middle of the street. The headline said: HISTORIC QUAPAW FIGURE TRIES TO PUT THE BITE ON LOCAL MATRON. I got Mom to save that paper. Zero is gonna love it!

"In the meantime, Edie is circulating another petition down at the mall to have Grandmother disarmed and locked up."

"Is there any danger of that?"

"None. The Governors Hillary and Billary love her."

We're silent for a long moment, then he sighs, "I hate us being so far apart. Wish I had my hands on you. Right now."

"Lovely idea," I murmur.

"Whoa," he says, "you just made my nipples go hard. Don't you go getting all sexy-voiced on me unless you're prepared to follow through."

"Soon, love, I hope very soon."

"Gotta sit down," Zero mumbles. The short walk to Jarvis Collegiate has worn him out. The auditorium is packed. Tonight, the candidates for the New Democratic Party in the next civic elections will be chosen.

"Do you think Searcy's going to get his nomination?" Snookums is fretting.

"I think he's going to be hard to beat," I reply.

"Who else is running for Ward Six?" Zero asks.

"That nut-bar concert violinist that the party establishment is so excited about, and reliable old Norah Spewe."

"Norah Spewe is one of the most obnoxious people in this city," states Snookums. "She's anti-choice, homophobic, you name it. I have never figured out what she's doing in this party. She's a real nasty piece of work."

"And she'll get votes, too," adds Hoo Hoo, shaking her head, "simply because she's a woman."

"It looks like half of the lesbians and gay people in the neighborhood are here," observes Blaine. "Searcy is a very popular guy."

"Well, in a world made up of shitheads and good-time gals, our Searcy is very definitely a good-time gal," I tell him.

Millie scuttles up, clipboard in hand. "You boys make room in this row for Searcy. David, do you have your nominating speech clear?"

"Who's seconding the nomination?" inquires Blaine.

"Lola Ming from the Downtown Tenants' Association," replies Millie. "She'll arrive with Searcy. Now, look sharp. I want this to run like clockwork." She darts away to button-hole somebody by the stage.

There is a stir at the back of the hall. Then a rising chant of "Searcy! Searcy! Searcy!" He moves up the aisle, smiling, and waving, like he's the Queen Mother. He is surrounded by a contingent of lesbian and gay youth who enthusiastically keep up the chant. From the other side of the room, Norah Spewe glares darkly at the spectacle. The party establishment shift uneasily in their places on stage. Their candidate, the violinist, sits across the aisle from us clutching his speaking notes. He has a slightly addled grin.

Searcy collapses in the space we've left for him. He fans himself vigorously with a GO, GOLDBERG! GO! poster. Lola and the lesbian and gay youth gang fill the row behind us.

The chairperson calls the meeting to order. The process moves quickly. Candidates for the school board and the other downtown wards are selected. Ward Six has been left to the end. The organizers know it will be the climax of the evening.

The violinist is the first to speak. He has managed to mix up his notes. He becomes more incoherent as his cue cards slip out of his hands and float to the floor in front of the stage. Finally, he shrugs, gives a befuddled grin, and lapses into silence. After a moment, he thanks us for electing him and leaves the stage.

"The poor guy," Zero says. "He may be great on the concert stage, but that was very painful. The people who talked him into running really should be spanked!"

Norah Spewe follows. She stares directly at Searcy and warns the assembly about frivolous candidates. There are scattered hisses and boos. She wades further in, denouncing the growing conspiracy of homosexuals, transvestites, and lesbian-feminists, whom she maintains have hijacked the party. Shouts of anger resound throughout the auditorium.

"Sit down, you miserable crank!" yells Zero. I haven't seen him so agitated in weeks.

Nora stamps furiously from the stage. The chairperson restores order. Lola and I do our nominating spiels, then our candidate takes his leisurely time crossing the front of the stage and mounting the steps to the podium. The crowd is shouting, "Searcy! Searcy!" Like a true showbiz pro, he lets the chanting build, then silences his fans with an imperious wave of his heavily jeweled hand.

He delivers a great speech. I must admit to being amazed at his grasp of downtown parking and zoning bylaws. He ends with a stinging attack on homophobia within the party, and in the community in general. He calls on the assembly to choose him and finally select an openly gay person to City Council. He acknowledges the thunderous applause by blowing kisses with both hands as he leaves the stage.

The first round of balloting is over quickly. The chairperson announces: Searcy 292, the violinist 202, and Norah Spewe 100. Not a clear majority. Norah is dropped from contention. She storms from the hall with a handful of cronies.

Voting begins on the second ballot. Millie paces fretfully.

Performing Without a Net

Searcy sits fanning himself, looking supremely confident. The auditorium is like a sauna. There's a stir on stage as the final results are handed to the chair: Goldberg 344, the violinist 240. Most of the crowd is on their feet cheering and whistling. The chant, "Goldberg! Goldberg! No more shit!" rises throughout the auditorium.

Searcy heaves himself majestically to his feet and again takes to the stage. Party hacks descend on him to pump his hand. The chairperson, an active supporter of the violinist, yanks Searcy's arm up in the air, as though he's just won a prizefight. And so he has.

Searcy rolls his eyes as he disentangles himself from the sweaty embrace of the newly enthusiastic chair. He steps up to the podium. The crowd falls silent. Searcy lowers his eyes demurely, then looks up at the crowd.

"Thank you all, so very, very much," he whispers huskily into the mike.

"What a shameless ham!" I groan.

"But what a pro," says Zero.

"There'll be no stopping the diva now," adds Snookums.

Searcy switches off the mike, steps back from the podium, plants his feet apart, puts his hands on his hips, and belts out, "I Am What I Am" from the musical *La Cage aux Folles*. The crowd is immediately on its feet singing with him. He leaves the stage and strides up the aisle, singing and waving. At the rear exit he pauses, throws a two-handed kiss, and is out the door. The crowd is delirious.

Millie wanders over, shaking her head. She looks like she's just been mugged. "None of that was planned."

"What a performance!" marvels Zero.

Millie shakes her head, "I'm not sure it will win an election."

"I think it just might," I say.

"And, precious, City Hall will never be the same again," chortles Snookums.

Zero is suddenly very pale. "You look tired, hon," I say, offering him a hand up.

LABOUR OF LOVE

"Don't mother me, David!" he snaps. But he does take my hand. Millie takes his other arm.

"I'll walk home with you," she offers. "I'm too pooped to party."

"So am I," says Zero weakly. "Is Searcy celebrating?"

"No," says Snookums. "He's going right home to crash. This has been a crazy week, even for him. Blaine and I are meeting the Bermuda Triangle at The Rose, if anyone wants to join us."

The rest of us pass. Zero's gone completely ashen. I'm anxious to get him home.

I get up late, which is unusual for me. Zero's already stretched out on the couch. He's been reading the paper but seems to be asleep. I don't want to wake him.

"What are you creeping around for?" he demands.

"Thought you were asleep."

"Not asleep. Thinking. Remembering."

"Jeff?" I ask.

"Yes, it was a year ago today."

"Are you okay?" I sit beside him.

"As okay as I can be. Jeff Lake was the hottest, sweetest connection to happen in my life since the first years you and I were together." He shakes his head. "I loved him very much, David, but it was different."

"I know that, hon."

"And then he was gone. Literally, in a puff of smoke."

It was so incredibly bizarre, so *National Enquirer*. I'd always wanted to know the details, but was reluctant to ask. We all were. So we all avoided it. We'd lost our friend, and Zero's lover, in this spectacular mishap, but for the most part, we sort of pretended it never happened. How many people do you know who've spontaneously combusted?

Performing Without a Net

Jeff had gone up in smoke at his piano while Zero was in the bathroom one hot, airless afternoon last summer.

Jeff had been sitting at his piano in the faded pink gym shorts he always wore around the apartment. Zero leaned over him to see what he was practicing. It was Ravel's "Pavane for a Dead Princess." He had been practicing that piece, trying to get it right, since their first night together. Zero kissed the top of Jeff's head and told him that he'd start dinner as soon as he went to the can. Jeff looked up, preoccupied, and smiled.

When Zero started back down the hall, there was an incredibly bright flash of light from the living room and a smell like brimstone laced with heliotrope and orange blossoms. In the seconds it took for Zero to get back down the hall, it was all over.

The piano bench was gone and so was Jeff. There was a tiny pile of light ashes. There weren't even any smoke stains!

Zero called me immediately. He was in shock. Deep shock.

"I thought that day and that week would never ever end," he says, shaking his head.

I can tell, even now, that the idea of it exhausts him.

"Police, forensic experts, scientists, the press. My tabloid life! Thank god y'all were here."

He looks thoughtfully out the window. "You know, I do miss him terribly, and it broke my heart, but I'm glad he went the way he did. He always said that's how he wanted to go. Here one moment; gone the next. And the KS they found in his lungs was spreading. Fast.

"Yeah, I lost him, but at least I had him. At least we found each other for a while.

"But, I do think about him all the time, and Randy, and all the other guys who were here and are gone. You."

"Me? I'm not gone."

"And what would I do if you were?"

"You'd carry on, Zero."

61

LABOUR OF LOVE

"David, I just can't imagine my world without you in it. We've been together for a long time." He shrugs. "Yeah, I know, give or take a Clay or a Jeff here or there, or Lance, or a hundred others. But think about it, except for the five months with Clay, we've shared a home since the moment we met. And despite my endless complaining, I never really wanted to be anywhere else."

"I guess, I always knew that, Zero."

"It's taken me a long time to understand. Our time together has always been so complex, so rich, so difficult. The time with Jeff is really like a dream. Unreal. Sometimes, it's almost like it didn't happen. We never had a cross word for each other, we just floated along together, happy in each moment.

"And there was none of the wear and tear I've always found in trying to build relationships while in the throes of new passion and romance."

I smile reflectively, thinking about our own throes of passion and romance those many years ago. They had been dreamlike, too, although some of those dreams had been nightmares!

"It sure wasn't like our first years together," he says, reading my mind.

"You were just a kid," I remind him.

"I was such a brat," he giggles, "such a spoiled princess. I don't know how you put up with me."

I smile. "Quite frankly, I don't know either. Glad I did, though."

"Even after all I've put you through?" he asks.

"Even after. I guess I'm just a bugger for punishment. And I really have been in love with you from the moment I first met you at Randy's front door."

"It was first sight for me, too," he reminds me. "There's sure been a lot of water under a lot of bridges since then. And there's still more to come. That's where I envy Jeff. The fucking virus didn't get him. He beat it. Made a clean getaway."

Performing Without a Net

"Yeah, I know what you mean," I say. "We should all be so lucky."

Edie calls at the stroke of twelve. "Hi y'all! We're here!"

"We?" I ask with some trepidation.

"Well, Doll's been working much too hard at Cohn's. It's tough being the manager of the biggest retailer in the city. And it's tougher for her since she's so young, and a woman. She had a couple of vacation days owing her, so I just brung her along. Now how's my boy?"

"He's sleeping right now. He's a little under the weather."

"Well, wake him up! I want to tell him about my plans for dinner."

"Sorry, Edie, no can do," I say firmly. "Why don't you give me your number at the hotel, and as soon as he wakes up, I'll have him call. He's really looking forward to seeing you," I lie.

"Well, we wanted to come over right now!"

"You can, but we'll just have to visit out in the garden until he wakes up."

"Oh, okay. We'll see you in a few minutes."

Zero appears at the door just as I hang up. He's dressed for the first time in two days.

"They're back," I tell him.

"They?"

"She brought Doll. They're on their way over."

He looks dreadful. He moves across the room to the couch like he's walking under water. He lies down and closes his eyes.

Edie's twang pierces the afternoon stillness as she vigorously rattles the front door handle. "Howdee, y'all! We're here!"

LABOUR OF LOVE

I take a deep breath and open the door.

"David!" she shrieks. She grabs me and kisses the air vigorously on both sides of my face, before swooping down on Zero.

Doll, bringing up the rear, gives me a solid hug. Her perfume is overwhelming. My eyes burn. Tears pour down my face. I guess she thinks I'm moved deeply by the sight of her. This provokes her to tears as well and she grapples me even closer into her poisonous aura. Fearful of some sort of toxic shock, I wrest myself from her fervent embrace.

"Good to see you, Doll. It's a nice surprise," I gasp.

"Zero!" Edie screams, "You look terrible! So do you, David. You look like cadavers!"

"Hi, Mom," Zero murmurs. "Please, don't start in on us. It's hard enough as it is, without you pointing out the obvious. Okay?"

"Well, pardon me for caring," she pouts, kissing the air around his face as well.

Doll sits beside him and gives him a hug.

His eyes immediately begin to redden and flow.

"It's okay, honey, it's okay," she says as she attempts to console him with another fragrant clinch. He dodges away, lurching to his feet to move weeping to the armchair across the room. Doll, satisfied, I guess, with all the deep emotional response she's triggered, settles back on the sofa with a serene smile.

"Well, I am here to fatten you up," Edie declares defiantly.

"Fattening up is not the issue, Mom. We have AIDS, remember?"

She ignores him. "You just let your old mother take care of you."

He rolls his eyes.

"I've booked us a table at Splendido for eight-thirty tomorrow night," she reports.

"But Mom . . ."

"My treat!"

Performing Without a Net

"These days we're usually going to bed at that hour," I point out.

"Oh," she says dismissively, "you boys need to get out and live a little. Besides, I have Sparky's gold card. The sky's the limit! And tonight we're gonna eat Arkansas. Show 'em the goods, Doll."

Doll dutifully rises and opens the huge tote bag she's lugged up the steps from the street. It's packed tight with containers full of fried chicken, collard greens, corn bread, lady peas, and all the fixings.

"Lutherette whipped up everything just before we left," Edie chirps. "I wanted to bring you home-cooked."

The sight and smell of his favorite Southern foods bring a smile to Zero's face. "Can't wait for supper," he says.

"I still can't believe how awful y'all look," Edie continues to chatter.

"Mom, leave it alone," Doll intervenes.

Edie sits back in the big armchair. "Now, how about that drink you haven't offered us yet?"

"Scotch?" I ask.

"Why, yes, that'd be real good."

"Doll?"

"The same."

I pour their drinks.

"You're not having a drink with us? Why not just a weenie little toast?"

"It's just not good for us these days, Mom," Zero reminds her.

"Party poopers!" she declares.

"You wouldn't believe what happened at the airport. The nicest gentleman with the cutest dog asked us if we were sisters."

Doll smiles bravely. "Tell the whole story, Mom."

"I just did, baby," says Edie, smiling very sweetly at her.

Doll looks at her and shakes her head. "The guy was blind, Mother."

65

Edie shrugs her shoulders and barrels on, "Who cares? I thought it was a real nice thing for him to say."

"Nice for you," Doll replies. "I don't care how good you look for your age, Mom, it does absolutely nothing for my ego to have my looks compared to those of a sixty-two-year-old."

"Oh, don't be so all-fired sensitive, missy," sniffs Edie. "Now, we came all the way up here to help y'all, and though Doll has to get back right away, I am prepared to stay as long as you need me."

"A few days will be fine," Zero replies.

"I don't know, son, you really look like you need me," she persists.

"I don't need you, Mom. And I don't want to be ridden about my health. Can't we just have a visit?"

"As usual, pardon me for caring." She drains her scotch, and gathers up her purse. "Well, we've said hi!, Doll. Let's get on back to the Sutton Place and have us a nap. Besides, Sparky and Harry are supposed to call."

Zero perks up. Fresh news. "Who's Harry?" he asks.

"Oh, Doll's new beau," Edie announces. "Harry Honeyfat, Junior." Doll blushes a furious scarlet.

"And I think I'm hearing weddin' bells!" Edie is beside herself at the prospect.

"Maybe you've just got a problem with your inner ear," Zero ventures. "Harry Honeyfat, Junior?" he muses. "Didn't you have an affair with Harry Honeyfat, Senior? Isn't he the one who used to phone you from his garden shed and talk dirty?"

"Zero! I never . . ." Edie chokes.

Doll is mortified.

"Just asking," says Zero with an innocent smile.

Edie's on her feet and heading for the door. "Come on now, Doll. I really need that nap. I'm plum tuckered." There are no good-bye air-kisses, just a little wave over her shoulder as they scoot out the door. Doll's aromatic presence lingers.

"Nice visit," I say.

Zero shakes his head. "This is not going to be an easy few days."

"Few days? She sounds like she's planning to be here for a while."

"She says that, but she doesn't really mean it," he replies. "You know how long her attention span is. She'll get distracted. Sparky will call with tickets to one of their haunts in the Caribbean or something, and she'll be gone so fast your head will spin."

"Well, I hope he calls soon." I yawn. "She's already worn me out."

We stretch out together, nerves on edge. Sleep will not come.

This time, Edie doesn't even bother to rattle the door. She just sails in. "Now, y'all just don't do anything. I am going to make you a good old Southern dinner."

"From scratch?" asks Zero.

"Yes, and no. I told you Lutherette helped out a bit. We just have to heat the collard greens and warm up the lady peas. Could you do that, Doll, while I scare us up some cocktails?"

"Sure, Mom, just love your home cookin'," mutters Doll, trudging into the kitchen.

Zero nods off. I get up to go to the bathroom. Edie follows me down the hall. She grabs my arm and hisses, "What is happenin'?" Her long, red fingernails dig into my flesh.

I think, Cruella De Ville; I think, Joan Crawford; I think, You're hurting my arm.

I tell her, "Zero isn't well. You know that. He really needs to conserve his energy. He's pushed himself very hard to finish his new book."

"He's written another book?" She seems flabbergasted.

"Yeah, and it's very good. You should be proud of him."

"I suppose," she says, screwing up her face. "I just wish he'd stop writing about me all the time."

"It's all fiction, Edie."

"Well, fiction or not, I also don't think there's any reason for him to keep writin' about us as though we had nothin' but a paranoid nose for trouble and an insane need to feed. Not to mention the sex. Why does he feels the need to include all that filthy sex? Nobody wants to know!"

"Somebody sure wants to know. A lot of people are buying the first novel."

"Anyway, David, I didn't ambush you here to discuss literature. Is he going to be all right?"

"He might be. I hope so, but it's unlikely. And he does not want to hear you go on about it. Do you understand that?" I'm trying not to be unkind.

"But I am his mother!" She tightens her grip on my arm. "And you just don't understand what it means to be a mother. I am here to help my little boy. I am prepared to be here as long as he needs me."

This is Zero's worst nightmare.

"Thanks, Edie, but I think we can manage. We will let you know the moment we need you."

"Mom!" Doll hollers from the kitchen. "Have you poured that damned drink yet? I'm gettin' mighty parched in here."

Edie releases my arm. "We'll talk later," she says conspiratorially. "Remember, David, I'm here for you, too."

Scary. Very scary. Somehow that pledge seems more of a threat than a promise.

After the dishes are cleared, they head back to their hotel. We head for bed. We've just tucked ourselves in when Edie calls.

"Doll is leaving in a few minutes. There's a crisis at the store."

"Can't it wait a day?" I ask. "Surely, Cohn's can survive this crisis without her. Zero will be so disappointed. He's hardly seen her."

"Doll has responsibilities as general manager," she informs me, "and she takes them very seriously. She'll call him from home."

Doll takes the phone. "I'm so sorry about this, David. Tell my brother I love him and I'll come back soon," she lowers her voice and whispers, "alone."

Edie calls about seven-thirty. It's an ungodly hour even for me. She cuts off my protests, "Now don't y'all argue with me this morning, David. I want you to get Zero up. Tell him I'll be right over. I have very important business to discuss with him. Alone."

"This is crazy! He's exhausted after that huge meal last night. Couldn't you just give him a few more hours?"

"You're always trying to keep me from my son," she accuses. "Well, it won't work this morning." She hangs up.

I go to the back to warn Zero. He's lying awake. I tell him his orders and her accusations. He's upset. "She's crazier than my dad."

He moves slowly about the room. He barely has time to establish himself on the couch with his coffee before she's at the front door, shouting "Howdee!" and rattling the knob.

I let her in, then make myself scarce out in the garden. I start to transplant some nicotiana on the cool, shady side of the deck. They'll smell heavenly in the evenings once they get established.

Edie is talking in the loud, overwrought stage-whisper she adopts whenever she thinks she's being intimate.

"Zero, have you changed your will?"

"No, Mom," he replies wearily. "Why would I? I told you ten years ago that I left everything to David. I don't see any reason to change that now."

"I just don't know how you can leave everything to a stranger!"

"David is not a stranger, Mom!" he protests. "I've spent most of my adult life with him. He practically raised me. And he's loved me unconditionally through all of my shenanigans. It's true, I have complained about him through the years, but when all is said and done, I love him. He's my family."

Edie snorts. "He is not your family, Zero! I am. I am your mother. I am responsible for who you are."

"Mom, I turned out okay in spite of you."

"But what about real family?" She can't leave it alone.

"I have built myself a real family, Mom, and David's at the heart of it." I can hear him trying very hard to be patient.

"You are impossible!" she fumes, her voice rising. "After all I've done for you . . ."

"Mom, you didn't even call when Jeff died. You didn't even bother to learn Clay's last name."

"Well, I can't be expected to do everything, can I? You are so mean! I want you to give serious thought to correcting that will, Zero. Family is important and you know, among other things, Doll sure would love to have those peacock dinner plates when you go."

"Mother!" He's angry.

"All right, I'm going, but think about it. I'll pick y'all up later for our fabulous dinner date." Sometimes she really sounds like a bad drag queen.

I wait until I hear her clatter out, then I go into the house.

"Did you hear any of that?"

"Most of it." I sit and put my arm around him.

He lies back on the couch. He can barely keep his eyes open. "The buzzards are beginning to circle."

We come to a jarring stop in front of Splendido. The drive over has been fast and terrifying.

I help Zero from the car. He reaches for me, off-balance. I take his arm. Edie waits impatiently for me to find some money for the valet parking.

Performing Without a Net

She's bubbling with chatter. Doll arrived safely back in Little Rock. The crisis has been averted. Sales staff in Hair Ornaments had been feuding for months over commissions. This had finally escalated into a major brawl, a fistfight in front of customers. With the wisdom of Solomon, Doll fired everyone in the department on the spot. She told them that there was plenty more low-life where they came from. The health of Hair Ornaments is extremely important to Doll. It's where she got her start at Cohn's.

"I tell you, Zero, you should be very proud of her. Your sister's gonna end up owning that store before she's finished. Mark my words. She's got 'corporate success' written all over her." Edie prattles on, barely pausing for breath.

We're led to our table. Zero leans heavily against me. I am very, very tired. Edie immediately orders herself a glass of champagne.

"Yes," she continues, "I have quit drinking, but champagne doesn't really count now, does it? All those bubbles make it more like soda pop, don't you think?"

"Yeah, sure, Edie," I say distractedly. Zero is ashen. He holds my hand very hard. Edie is on her fourth "soda pop" when our meals arrive.

Zero slumps in his chair. "David," he whispers, "I've got to get home."

He pulls himself up in his chair, then attempts to stand. He pitches over on to his head. Hard.

Edie screams. She knocks back the rest of her champagne, then screams again. Waiters converge.

Zero is not unconscious. He's struggling to get up. The maître d', full of concern, helps me to lift him from the floor. Already a huge bruise spreads like a wine-stain over Zero's temple.

Edie is grabbing at my arm. "What are we gonna do? What are we gonna do!" she wails.

I can hear the rising note of hysteria in her voice. I want to keep this calm. "First, you're going to take some deep breaths, then you are going to get the parking valet to bring the car around to the front, then you are going to drive us carefully to Sunnybrook Hospital. Have you got that? Now hurry."

"Can I use your phone?" I ask the maître d'. He's back in an instant with a cordless from behind the bar. I find my emergency numbers and call Dr. Susan Fieldstone at home. One of her children answers. I ask for her mom. Susan's just walked in the door.

"Tell her it's David McLure and it's an emergency." Dr. Fieldstone picks up the line. She sounds very tired. I tell her the score.

"Bring him right up to emergency. I'll meet you there," she says.

"Thanks, Susan," I say as she hangs up.

Edie comes back into the restaurant. She's weeping.

I ask the waiter, "Can you help me get my friend to the car?"

"Sure, man," he's quick to respond.

Zero clutches his forehead. He moans softly. The waiter and I put our arms around him. There seems to be no resistance in his legs. He can't stand alone. We walk him slowly to the door through the startled herd of grazing yuppies. They all pretend nothing is happening. The distraction is studiously ignored.

Edie opens the doors. She slouches behind the steering wheel, tapping her nails on the dashboard, while the waiter and maître d' settle us in the backseat. Zero's head is cradled in my lap. "Thanks, guys. You've been great. Now, Edie, let's get to Sunnybrook. Dr. Fieldstone will meet us there."

She looks at me with exasperated disdain, "Well, aren't you going to tip the valet?"

THE FAT LADY SINGS

D r. Fieldstone ushers me into her too-familiar office. I know what's coming. "I've taken all the therapies as far as I can and he's not responding, David. So I'm sending him home. Tomorrow."

Yes, I knew this was coming. Still, I'm not ready. I feel like she's just sucker-punched me. And she has.

"We'll get you in touch with Paul Cotes, the palliative care doctor, and, of course, if Zero has a seizure at home, you could still bring him in here. Otherwise . . ."

"Otherwise what, Dr. Fieldstone? We're on our own now? Can you at least tell me what to expect?" I fight a wave of panic.

She wants this conversation to be over. "It's hard to predict," she says, "more of the same. Just take it a day at a time."

I am confused and angry. "Surely you can give me some idea about how toxo usually progresses?"

"Can't really," she shakes her head, turning away. "Cotes is good, and you'll cope." She comes over and gives me a perfunctory, little hug. "It's hard, I know, David, but it's time to let him go."

"Fine, but what do I do between now and when he's gone?" And afterward?

* * *

75

LABOUR OF LOVE

I go back up to D4, the AIDS ward, before heading home. When I come into the room he turns and gives me a mild smile. He's thumbing through *Vanity Fair*. There's a piece about William Burroughs. He reads me a bit. Tells me a weird anecdote about staying at Burrough's bunker on the Bowery in Manhattan years ago.

Zero had just met Randy at some Broadway opening and they had been swept up in an after-show party that had eventually deposited them at Burrough's place. The anecdote has to do with Burrough's obsession with firearms. Before retiring for the night, he had shown Randy and Zero a number of bizarre weapons upon which he seemed to lavish quite a paranoid affection. He assured them that any intruder into his home would be in deep and serious trouble. The lights were put out and the boys huddled together the rest of the night, afraid to use the bathroom for fear that Burroughs might mistake them for cat burglars and mow them down. He's told me this tale before. There's always some new, crazy detail. Classic Zero. I've always found it funny. Today, my mind is racing a million miles away.

"She's sending you home."

He nods. He knows.

"She says the therapies aren't working."

"That's clear," he replies. He shrugs. "But what can we do?" He's quiet for a long time, his head on my shoulder. I think he's dozed off. "I still want to finish this at home," he says, "with you."

"It's a deal."

"No hospice?"

"No hospice," I assure him.

"Can you handle all this?"

"We'll manage, sweetheart," I promise. I laugh. "Or die trying."

Lucy and I go out to Sunnybrook to pick him up, first thing in the morning.

The Fat Lady Sings

He's dressed and packed. Anxious to be home. He sits on the edge of the bed, looking out at the bright, hot sky. He wears a look of bemused concentration like he's straining to identify some elusive sound in the far distance. It's a look he's worn often through this hospital stay. Through these interminable weeks. Through this wild, nightmare roller coaster of gnawing infection and drugs. Through this losing game of chance.

It's a look that seems to signal that he's somehow pulled out and away from the daily toxic encroachment that hems him in.

He seems to have found a quiet, safer place to be. A haven in his beleaguered mind. It's not that he's less alert or less aware. Rather, it's a loss, somehow, of an emotional edge. As though the anger and impatience that have always animated him have disappeared. In many ways there is something quite beautiful about this new tranquillity. But it is disconcerting as well.

Some of the nurses at the station look up, smile, say good-bye. They know he's being sent home to die. Lucy and I put our arms around him and start the long walk down the hall.

On the way down Mount Pleasant he holds tightly to my hand, but doesn't speak. Lucy fills us in on the neighborhood gossip. I'm thankful for her chatter. There is too much in my head.

Can we make this work? Do I have enough energy to see this through? Will our friends be there when push comes to shove? Endless what ifs . . . Too many questions. No answers.

Lucy and I each take an arm to help him into the house. The garden is in glorious bloom. His face lights up when he sees it.

"I want to sit out here on the deck," he announces.

We help him settle in his rocker, then Lucy heads back to the archives. "Thanks a lot, Luce," he says.

"Yeah, thanks a lot," I echo.

"Oh, David," she asks, stopping at the door, "does this mean our dinner date with Frenchie is off for tonight?"

LABOUR OF LOVE

"Don't cancel because of me," says Zero. "I'd love to go for dinner. I've been on hospital cuisine for weeks. I'd happily eat dirt at this point."

"Okay, guy, if you're up for it. We'll pick you up about six-thirty. I'll call down, though, ahead of time to see if you still feel like doing it."

"Great, Lucy. Thanks again." I give her a hug.

I join Zero on the deck.

"It's so good to be home," he sighs.

"It's so good that you're back. Everyone is anxious to see you, but I've tried to set up a schedule so we're not being swamped with visitors. Snookums, Searcy, and Lucy have been busy organizing a care team for us. There's a meeting tomorrow at the 519 Community Centre to get everyone briefed and introduced. Paul Cotes, the palliative care doc, will be there. You know, we have more than fifty people signed up to give us a hand."

"I guess we were smart to start preparing for this when we did," he says.

Last winter, when both our conditions had begun to deteriorate at once, Zero had suggested we collect people's numbers when they offered to help. Now when we need them, contacting them is relatively easy. And we need them.

"Your mom's been calling," I report. "She wants to come back soon."

He groans and shakes his head, "No, no, no, no, no."

Edie had left in a royal huff several days after Zero's admission to the hospital. For the first days following his collapse in the restaurant, he was quite confused. Edie had decided at that point that he was more or less brain-dead. She would hold forth in tragic tones to anyone who would listen that this was not her Zero. This was a vegetable. "Why, it's like talking to a plate of okra!" she'd announce tearfully. The tragedy you were to understand was hers, not Zero's.

Despite her contention that he was no longer capable of logical thought, she continued to harass him about the contents of his will and his funeral instructions. He was unyielding. This continued resistance to her attempts to subvert his wishes only served to solidify her conviction that he had indeed taken full leave of his senses. The logic being that if he didn't agree with her, then it was obvious he must have lost his mind.

Finally, he told the staff on the ward that he couldn't take it anymore. They contacted the hospital social worker and Dr. Fieldstone and asked if there was some way Edie could be asked to leave. They felt she was exhausting Zero and driving him, and everyone else, mad in the process.

Dr. Fieldstone, a mother herself, asked Zero and me if we really wanted Edie to go. She would tell her to if that's what we wanted. Zero said she had to go. I agreed. The message was relayed.

And she left. But not graciously. Her departure involved a tearful and high-pitched denunciation, delivered to the entire ward, of our callous disregard for the sacred flower of Southern motherhood. The staccato flurry of her furious stilettos when she finally made her exit was greeted with a collective sigh of relief and a hearty round of applause.

"She's been calling here a lot," I report.

"She's been calling me at the hospital, too. I really think she wants to help. She offered to pay my share of the rent. She's sending a check to cover it."

"Good for her," I say. Hard-nosed and skeptical, as always, I'll believe it when I see it.

The meeting room at the 519 Church Street Community Centre is crowded. Old friends, new friends, friends of friends. We introduce ourselves.

I thank them for coming, then brief them on Zero's current condition. Dr. Cotes tells them about toxoplasmosis, what services and resources are available, what to do in an emergency. Any questions?

The finality of embarking on this last journey with Zero is tough for me. For all of us.

I am brimful with raw pain. It washes through me, lapping at the surface of my calm. I struggle to keep from being submerged.

I tell them to remember that, barring some miracle, it probably is time for Zero to go. Our purpose is to see him safely and soundly through to the end, however that might come, whenever that might be. There will be no heroic procedures to prolong his life. Death is an acceptable outcome.

It's nearly too hard to say those words. I choke on them. Even my best friends must look away. On either side of me, Hoo Hoo and Snookums slip their arms around me. Hold me tight between them. Tears spill, silent and corrosive, down my face. The team members are quiet, preoccupied, as they file out.

When everyone else is gone, Dr. Cotes sits down with me. Earlier, he had visited the house and spent an hour with Zero.

"How do you think he's doing?" I ask.

"It's clear the toxo has damaged him badly."

Last night Zero fell again. He can no longer sit or stand without help. He's bigger than me. I'm already completely worn out and I guess I look it.

"Just play it a day at a time, David," says Paul. "It's going to change all the time and it's going to get worse. You have to look after yourself. You look terrible and you'll be no damn good to anyone if you collapse, too.

"You're the linchpin. The primary care-giver. The rest of us can come and go, but you'll be here through it all. And this care team can't do its job without you."

"Yeah, I know."

"Yes, you know, but you're still not going to slow down, are you?" He shakes his head in exasperation.

The Fat Lady Sings

"I'm trying; I really am. My fear, though, is that if I stop, even for a minute, I'll never get started again."

"I know that feeling, but you still have to try for his sake. And for yours."

"Goodnight, Frenchie. Thanks," I say. I give back the Tupperware she's used to deliver our dinner. Snookums lingers.

"Are you okay, precious?" he inquires.

"Totally wasted, but it could be worse." I manage a grin.

He sits down on the couch and pats the cushion beside him. "Sit."

"Just let me check to see if he's okay. I'll be right back."

"No! Zero is all right. You sit down here. Now!" he orders.

I obey.

"Now, lie down with your head in my lap. You need some serious care, precious." He caresses my scalp, my face. He sings softly. It's a Trinidadian lullaby. I slip into blessed sleep on the soft lilt of his childhood patois:

> "Do, Do, p'ti popo
> p'ti popo pa vle dodo
> gwo booboola bi manger ou . . ."

I am vaguely aware of the phone ringing. Snookums is in murmured conversation with someone. When he begins to shout I stumble, dazed, into consciousness.

In all the years of our friendship, I have never seen Snookums so enraged before.

"How can you say that, Mrs. MacNoo? Zero may not be his usual self, but he is not dead! He's still very much alive and he's still enjoying life! He is not a vegetable! He deserves more respect from you." He listens to her response. "Of course, I know what I'm talking about!" he sputters angrily. "He loves the garden, the flowers, the music. Books. His friends. Being home. He has a great appetite. Yes, there is still lots of quality in his life. And besides, it will be his decision to continue if he wants. You just can't . . ." He stops in mid-sentence. I know she's hung up on him. He stares at the receiver a moment, then hangs up, too.

He's flushed and a bit out of breath. "Sorry, precious. I'm afraid I lost it with old Blanche Dubois there. She really sounds like she's already written him off and is anxious not to have him linger on. She kept mentioning hearing wedding bells. I get the impression she figures he'd be in the way if that sister of his gets married.

"Anyway, she sure pushed all of my buttons. I hope I never have to speak with her again. Moments like this make me I wish I had never taken the pledge."

"Sorry, Snookums. You shouldn't have to deal with her."

He shrugs. "Nobody should have to."

It's strange. I don't question for one moment that she loves Zero very much, and that she's full of grief, in anticipation of his death. But, at the same time, there is something so self-indulgent about her histrionics. And heaven forbid that any of this should really interfere with her social life or inconvenience her in any real way.

She continues to agitate to be allowed to visit. Zero continues to insist that Labor Day will be soon enough. She complains bitterly, but I think she's relieved.

Doll calls in a state of ecstasy. Zero is still asleep.

"I'm getting married!" she squeals. "And I want both of you to be there. Besides, this should get Mom off your backs for a while."

"That's wonderful, Doll. Congratulations. Who are you marrying?" I am truly pleased for her.

"Harry Honeyfat, Junior. He's the credit manager at our store. Listen, I'll call you again later when Zero is awake. Whatever you do, don't tell Mom that I told you guys first. She'll kill me if she ever finds out she wasn't the first I told."

"My lips are sealed."

"Thanks, David. Just act surprised when she calls you with the news. Oh, and David," she adds, as an afterthought, "I'm coming up there sometime in the next few days."

"What!"

"Didn't Mom tell you? She was supposed to."

I tell Zero the news.

"I know they mean well, but I don't want to see any of them," he whispers. "No, that's wrong. I do want to see them, but only for about fifteen minutes. They sit around looking at me like a bunch of doleful old hounds. It's just too exhausting.

"And wait till they see me in the wheelchair. What's that utterly charming term Mom uses for people with disabilities? 'Horribly crippled'? Yes, that's it. Well, now along with everything else, they'll have to grapple with me being 'horribly crippled' as well."

This is a long speech for him these days. Almost a rant, delivered in the small, breathy whisper that's become his speaking voice.

He goes for much of the day now in silence. Our communications are largely through instinct. A shift of the eyes. A raised brow. Small smiles. One raised finger for "yes," two for "no."

He is increasingly serene. The acerbic wit, the restless, demanding energy, the temper so often characteristic of his interaction with the world, have vanished. Zero has moved to a state of peace. His brow never furrows. The doctor says that he is feeling no pain. He seems fully aware, loving, articulate, though he speaks less with each passing day.

I, on the other hand, am running on empty, running on love alone. I feel battered and invaded by the constant traffic. Nurses, homemakers, family, friends, the care team volunteers, throng through the house. The parade begins at dawn, and continues until late into the night. There is no privacy, no respite, no place to hide. To get the care we need, we surrender our home, our time, our secrets, to the world. Often to complete strangers. It's a devil's deal.

Zero's condition changes daily. Deteriorates. The day is filled with constant tasks. He must be lifted, carried, fed, medicated, diapered, cleaned. He suffers all of this with great dignity and without complaint. His appetite is voracious. He spends most of his waking hours reading magazines or gazing at the flowers that fill the yard. Lucy comes, every day, to read aloud to him from Margaret Laurence's *The Diviners*.

Friends from the care team come in the evening to give him dinner, change his dressings, put him to bed. Every afternoon, Carlotta, a nurse from the complex care program, comes by. She is a warm and glowing presence. Sometimes she and Zero will sit all afternoon in complete silence. She will not leave at the end of her shift unless he gives her a smile. He always does.

Nights and mornings are harder. Much harder. He is totally incontinent. The entire bed linen must often be changed four or five times through the night. I think I cannot do it again, but then I do, because I have to.

We are in a desperate battle to contain his bedsores. Bedsores he developed in the hospital, where skin care seems to be a completely foreign concept. The constant cleaning and redressing of the sores is the hardest task for me. I'm sure I'm hurting him, but the doctor tells me that isn't so. Zero never once complains.

Through it all I keep talking. It's a monologue, primarily, since he rarely speaks. We always maintained that we lived in a musical comedy and now I sing and dance for him. I try to keep him smiling. The show must go on.

Once he's tucked in at night, and everyone else is gone, I crouch on the floor beside him, stroke his head, and sing lullabies till he sleeps. In the daytime, when we can find the time to be alone, I stretch out beside him on the bed and improvise soft little scat tunes. He sings his own back to me. It's silly and it's magical. And it delights us both.

The Fat Lady Sings

* * *

It's early. Zero asks to be out in the morning sun. I sit him up, and swing his legs to the floor. Lift his arms, and place them around my neck. Bend down, and wrap my arms around his torso.

"Okay, darling. Help me now. Let's lift together. Try to push yourself up with your legs and thighs." His arms tighten on my neck. "Let's go!" I urge, and in one heaving lift, he's on his feet, staggering against me. We lean against each other, winded, savoring the full contact, now almost impossible to achieve in bed, what with catheters, diapers, and bedsore dressings. He leans his head on my shoulder, kisses my neck.

"My one," I say.

"My only," he replies.

Moments of respite are rare, and too short. Millie, Hoo Hoo, Frenchie, and Lucy hoping to get me to slow down and relax, conspire constantly to lure me from the house.

Edie is unrelenting. She phones at all hours.

"I get some of Zero's ashes," she announces, without even bothering to say hello.

"What are you on about?" I mutter groggily. "Zero's never mentioned that to me, and he's given me very specific funeral instructions in writing."

"Well, we made an arrangement," she says smugly.

We are about to enter open warfare. "Was that before or after you decided he was brain-dead?" I ask sweetly. She snorts, and hangs up.

Later, I ask Zero. He grimaces and whispers, "You know Mom. In her fevered imagination, she's made an arrangement. I guess it's not real important."

LABOUR OF LOVE

* * *

News comes, mid-month, of a film option on the first book, and the sale of the new manuscript. A five-thousand-dollar writer's grant arrives in the mail. It's all late, but not too late. He knows how successful his work is. He tries to maintain his veneer of jaded, showbiz cynicism, but I can see he is so proud he could explode. And so am I.

Doll calls from the airport. She'll be in shortly. I'm in the middle of dressing Zero when I hear her knock. I shout that I'll be there in a minute. The knocking persists, becomes more insistent. By the time I've staggered from the bedroom with Zero and deposited him on the couch, the hammering is thunderous. The door shakes in its frame.

"Please, get her to stop," Zero moans, clutching his head.

Completely frazzled, I rush to the door and fling it open. Not a moment too soon. Doll seems about to launch herself in a final, wood-splintering assault.

She beams. "Hidee, David. Thought y'all might be asleep or something. You know, it's not polite to keep a lady waiting."

She hugs me, then throws her arms out in a wild flourish and shouts, "Surprise!"

Zero's father leaps out from behind the lilacs by the gate and does a crazy soft-shoe routine up the walk.

"Mom and I thought we'd surprise y'all by bringing Daddy."

I feel a bit unhinged. Charles, mugging up at me, is winding up a frantic buck-and-wing at the foot of the steps. "Surprise us. How thoughtful of you. Surprises are just what we don't get enough of around here."

"Yeah, that's what we thought," she says cheerily, barging past me, to deposit herself heavily on the couch beside Zero.

Charles hops up the steps and takes my hand, which he shakes firmly. He's freshly barbered, and wears a conservative, well-cut gray business suit. Around his neck is a chain constructed from paper clips. From the chain, a hand-lettered medallion swings. It says, "Lord High Mayor of Absolutely Nothing." The last two words are heavily underlined in red marking pen.

He puts his arm around me, and in a low voice says, "Listen, David, I am sorry about this. I told them the last thing you needed was surprises. But you know how far my opinions get with this crowd.

"I did want to see him, though. I hope I'm welcome."

I've always been fond of Zero's dad. He's often spectacularly crazy, but I also understand the haven that madness must provide. "Of course you're welcome, Charles. You know we've been trying to get you to visit us here since we moved. I just wish it were under better circumstances. Come on in."

I lead him into the living room. Zero gives him a sunny smile.

The visit passes in a blur. Doll is distraught over Zero, but preoccupied with wedding plans. Harry Honeyfat, Junior, beams, red-faced and portly, from the photographs. She claims she wants the wedding to be a modest little affair, but Edie has already decided on six bridesmaids. Doll, of course, is thrilled. No doubt she has visions of a gala to outstrip her thirtieth birthday, which culminated in the famous MacNoo Family Capital Hotel Shoot-Out.

Out of the mother/daughter outfits she and Edie traditionally traipse around in, Doll, in jeans and a sweatshirt, is a different person. Relaxed. Or as relaxed as you can get with your brother dying from lesions on his brain and your own head clanging with wedding bells.

The noxious scent from her last visit has been replaced by something pleasantly floral.

Charles is quite subdued and soft-spoken, anxious to know what's happening, eager to be of assistance. He tells terrible, lame jokes, which leave him shaking with helpless mirth, tears of merriment streaming down his ruddy cheeks.

LABOUR OF LOVE

He spins wonderful, rambling, gentle yarns mostly about his childhood.

At five years of age, he was taken by his father to St. Louis, Missouri, to see the great Babe Ruth play baseball. They saw the game from close up and Charles even got the Babe's autograph on a ball.

Later, they went for dinner at a grand hotel. Although there were great, lazy ceiling fans, the weather was extremely hot, and the room was stifling. Little Charles, overcome by the heat, the heavy food, and the excitement of the day, crawled under the table to rest, and soothe his distended little belly on the cool tiles at his father's feet.

A story like this can take hours. I find them totally charming. Zero points out that they do lose some of that charm after the first hundred times you hear them. No matter, though. It's certainly clear where Zero's knack for a tale comes from.

Zero speaks little while they're here, but smiles at them a lot. Holds their hands. Despite the initial shock, I'm glad they came. Glad, too, when they go. Energy is at a premium, and everybody in the house seems to drain me.

Zero's brother, Norm, finally calls. Can he bring his children, Rotten Dog and Little Cookie, to see their Uncle Zero before he dies? They think about him all the time. Besides, they'd like to see the Blue Jays play ball at the Sky Dome. Can I get them tickets? Next weekend would be most convenient. I pass this message on to Zero. He takes the phone. "Fuck off, Norm!" he whispers.

Edie's calls escalate. Become more bizarre, more demanding. Will Zero cut short all of this nonsense with pills? If he does, can she be there? I tell her no.

"But I want to be there," she whines.

"It's not your decision," I tell her.

The Fat Lady Sings

"But I can't stand him continuing in this condition," she wails.

"Well, that's too bad, Edie. If he does decide to end it, it will not be a spectator sport."

"You just don't understand what it means to be a mother," she accuses once again.

"Edie," I say, impatiently, "I have a mother and I've been at death's door myself a number of times. There are other ways to be a mother."

She's been in therapy for a while now, and, after a silence, she says, "Thank you for sharing that with me, David. Now, I know how much good work you've done, and how you care for Zero, so I'm going to try to remember those positive things when I think of you." Then abruptly, as always, she is gone.

I say, "Bye, Edie" to the dead line.

When Zero first fell ill, Edie had made extravagant claims to all who'd listen that she and Sparky would guarantee that her son had the best care available. I actually believed her until tonight. It's late and I've just changed the bedding for the third time. I'm exhausted, on the verge of tears. I'm afraid I'm going to unravel. Finally, I swallow my pride and call Little Rock.

"Edie, we need help. Do you remember your offer to get a nurse, if we needed one?"

"Well, yes," she answers guardedly.

"Well, I think we're going to need someone at night," I tell her.

I can almost actually hear her waffling. "Sparky and I will have to discuss it," she says.

"What's to discuss? This is your son we're talking about. You said you'd help. We need your help." I can feel my voice rising in anger.

"Like I say, we'll think about it."

"Thanks, Edie, you do that. Let me know."

LABOUR OF LOVE

"Okie dokie," she trills. She hangs up.

I know now that there will be no help from them. I feel so humiliated to have asked for help only to be turned down. Played with. So angry at even having to ask. I run a hot bath and sit in the tub, sobbing.

I'll get Searcy to call the care team together. We'll regroup. Get friends to help longer at nights. We'll get through.

It is bright and hot again this morning. Snookums, Blaine, Lucy Culpepper, and I are taking Zero on an excursion. We wrestle him in the wheelchair down the steps, then load him into Lucy's station wagon. He's not talking today, but is positively jolly, greeting everyone's valiant attempts to be funny with his lopsided little grin. He's happy to be on an adventure in the fresh air.

He and I are scrunched together in the backseat. I hum a little tune into his ear. He hums back. Squeezes my hand. Then he's distracted by all the action on the street. This is the first time he's been out since the hospital, other than to sit on the deck at home. He presses his face to the glass. Drinks it all in.

At the wonderful tangle of the wild garden by the Ecology Conservation House on Madison, we park and unload. He touches everything along the winding path in the little park. Leaves. Seed pods. Wild flowers. The grape vines snaking up the wall.

He plucks a grape, a long, hard task with those trembling fingers, rolls it between thumb and forefinger. Somehow lifts it to his mouth, pops it in, holds it there. He's very pleased with himself. His eyes are merry. There's a glint of sly accomplishment. He bites down, puckers with the burst of juicy tartness. Savors it.

After devouring the picnic that Blaine and Snookums have prepared, he indicates he wants to stroll up Bloor Street. As we roll him along, he eats an ice cream cone, smiling and waving in a truly queenly manner, to all we pass. By the time we reach the car, and get everything loaded, he's exhausted. He sleeps the whole way home.

Edie calls. She's found out through Doll that Zero received his latest writer's grant. She had, as promised, actually paid his rent for one month. "Now," she says, "I don't expect he'll be needing it. I don't want any of us to have financial difficulties in these troubled times."

I guess she figures his writer's grant has solved our money dilemma. When the grant is used up, as it will be any day now, I can then call her and plead for the rent check she'd promised her dying son. I, of course, have nothing else to do with my time. She likes to make you beg.

"If you do need the money, you will contact me, won't you?"

"Yeah, sure," I mutter. "But I'll kill myself first."

She tells me that Sparky would like to have a meal catered from the hotel when they're here over the Labor Day weekend. What would Zero like?

"He loves rack of lamb," I tell her, "and that might also be something he can still hold on to."

"Sounds good," she chirps.

I point out that members of the care team will be here as well, specifically Snookums, Searcy, and Frenchie. This news is greeted with silence. Then she says with exasperation, "I suppose that means we'll have to feed them, too?"

"Wouldn't hurt," I venture, biting back my anger.

I want to tell her that she could rent the ballroom at her damned luxury hotel and cater in rack of lamb for every member of the care team for the next month, and it would never begin to repay the totally unself-conscious and ceaseless giving our friends, our real family, provide us every day in caring for her son, and for me. But I rarely allow myself a full response. She'll only hang up. Often, too often, I've been left with a mouthful of unarticulated bile. I learn.

In cooler moments I do realize that she provides a clear, deserving focus for the often inchoate anger I feel at this whole hideous situation. Bumbling, confused bureaucracies, arrogant, ill-informed medicos, lunatic homemakers, frightening nurses, bad drugs, inappropriate equipment that always arrives five days too late.

And her behavior does throw into stark contrast the wonderful treatment we do receive from individuals in the care system, and the endless outpouring of love and kindness we receive from friends, family, and neighbors.

I dread their coming. I know their intent. Edie is consumed with guilt at not helping with Zero's care. After all, why would you invest good shopping money in someone you already regard as dead? She and Sparky will push to put Zero in the hospice. That way, his care would all be paid for, this is Canada after all, and they can stop feeling guilty for not helping. He'd be in an institution, so they can really forget him and get on with that wedding.

It's getting harder for Zero to talk at all. I need to check things out with him before they arrive. I know the weekend will be a battle. Carlotta helps me wheel him on to the deck. I squat down beside him and take his hand in mine.

"Sparky and your mom are coming tomorrow."

He rolls his eyes. There is a ghost of a smile.

"You know, they'll want to put you in the hospice?"

"Yes."

"Do you want to go?"

"No."

"Do you want to stay here, at home?"

"Yes."

The Fat Lady Sings

Then it's settled. His fingers tighten momentarily on mine. He's falling asleep in the bright sun.

They call from the hotel. They'll be over for lunch.

Zero refuses to speak to them or acknowledge them in any way. He will not allow eye contact. Edie contorts herself, trying to place herself in his line of vision. She keeps poking at him with those bright red nails, shrilling again and again, "Are you in pain? Are you in pain?" It's nightmarish.

Sparky sits on the couch, ignoring them both. He pontificates to Searcy, who was bred and born in Montreal, on the history of French and English relations in Canada. Since his unfortunate accident at the MacNoo Family Capital Hotel Shoot-Out, Sparky's voice has risen an octave. Despite his wife's best efforts to shoot his private parts off, they have remained intact, but severely traumatized. He sounds like Minnie Mouse.

Searcy gets me alone in the kitchen. "What a pompous asshole!" he fumes. "I feel like I'm trapped in a bad cartoon."

"That's because you are, Blanche," I assure him.

Searcy and Snookums rustle us up some dinner from leftovers in the fridge. Edie and Sparky watch us eat, but decline the invitation to join us. Finally, they leave. They have reservations at Il Fenice, a fine restaurant and one of their favorite haunts in Toronto. There has been no mention of Zero's rack of lamb. And I don't ask.

We are all barely civil. Zero visibly relaxes as the door closes behind them. Tomorrow will be another day. They'll be back.

Sparky, Edie, and I tour the hospice. They are clearly impressed, especially by the state-of-the-art hydrotherapy equipment. I point out that Zero still wants to stay at home. I assure them that we would

93

respect that wish. That all of us involved in his care felt we could do it. They glare at me with naked hostility. This is not their scenario.

As we leave the hospice, Sparky begins to stroke his beard and assumes his wise old crackerbarrel-philosopher look. Betcha it's pure dynamite in the corporate law courts where he makes his millions.

"David," he begins, "it's important, now, for Zero to acknowledge Death, then he can get on with the healing and the joy."

Healing? What healing? Did they find a cure while we were at lunch? What is this man saying? That they want Zero to commit suicide so they can get on with that miserable wedding?

"Well, Sparky, we have acknowledged Death. Right now, though, we're very busy acknowledging Life. Besides, what do you want me to do? Go home and shake Zero until he says, 'I acknowledge Death'? Then, what am I to do? Smother him with a pillow?"

Sparky glares at me. Edie is sniffling. We trudge along in silence. Edie, in an alarmingly bright, cheerful voice, suddenly suggests that we stop somewhere for a smart cocktail. Of course, there's our solution. Will this never end?

We find a table outside at The Old House On Church. As soon as we settle in and order drinks, she says, "Tell Sparky the plans."

"What plans?" I ask warily.

"For when Zero passes on, of course."

I take a deep breath and begin to outline the funeral arrangements Zero and I have made. Edie interrupts impatiently.

"No, no, no. I mean the ashes."

"Well," I tell them, "I did intend to take some of his ashes to Arkansas, but I can't guarantee how quickly that will happen. We kept my dad in a box on the porch for over a year, until we were all able to make it home."

"Well, boy, where we come from we like to get 'em in the ground, as soon as possible," Sparky squeaks, gruffly.

"Out of sight, out of mind, eh, Spark? What's the damned rush? It's not as though he's going to spoil." I am furious.

The Fat Lady Sings

"Oh, David, please, don't be difficult about this!" Edie cajoles.

I stand up and knock over my untouched Campari and soda. We walk back down Church Street in frosty silence.

Dr. Cotes, the palliative care doctor, meets them at the house in the morning. Sparky assumes he's found an ally. After all, Paul is a trained medical professional. He immediately launches into a high-pitched tirade.

"We want to get Zero moved to that hospice. We want him to have the very best care. But this young fellow," he points at me, guess he's forgotten my name, "seems to think he can take care of him."

"Well, he has, and I assure you that Zero is getting the best care possible." The anger in Paul's voice is controlled, but evident.

"Unfortunately, that's not how we feel," sniffs Edie.

"Fortunately, it's not your decision to make, Mrs. MacNoo. It's up to Zero and David. As long as Zero wants to be home, and David thinks he can manage it, this is where Zero will stay. On my strongest recommendation."

"Well, that's that, Edie." Sparky is livid. Unable to get his own way, he's not about to linger.

Edie slips into the bedroom to say her good-byes. Sparky doesn't bother. We won't be seeing them again. When Edie returns, sobbing, Sparky is already on his feet, impatient to leave.

She looks devastated. I feel genuinely close to her and the imminence of her grief. She hugs me and thanks me for all I've done. Then, she pulls me into the kitchen and hands me a list. "I made another arrangement with Zero. He wants these cherished objects to come to me." This is truly too twisted. My good feelings of a moment before evaporate.

"Edie," I say, "none of this is in his will. You'll get exactly what Zero has designated for you. I'm tired of hearing about your bogus arrangements." She's hyperventilating. I think, for a moment, that she might actually attack me.

"Let's go, Edie," Sparky pipes impatiently from the hall in his girlish treble.

Edie clatters down the steps. There are no good-byes. I lock the front door behind them.

I go in to see Zero immediately. He looks terrified. He's shaking violently. Paul holds his hand, and strokes his temples.

"It's okay, Zero, it's okay," he murmurs. "They're gone now. You're not going anywhere. You're going to stay right here."

We both talk to him and caress him until his eyes close and the trembling stops. His breathing is deep and raspy.

Paul gets up and leaves the room. I bend down and kiss Zero, then follow him.

"I'm ordering him a hospital bed," he says. "Those bed sores are terrible, and I don't think he should be moved anymore."

My heart breaks. Up to now, even with all the paraphernalia of catheters, pads, and diapers, I've still been able to curl up in some sort of contact with him. I know that once the hospital bed arrives, it's unlikely that I'll ever sleep with him again.

Paul makes the arrangements over the phone. He gives me a long hard hug. "It won't be long now," he says. As the door closes behind him, I sink to the floor beside my desk and cry.

I wake up with my face scrunched against the floor. It's already nearly noon. Carlotta will be here shortly. I stumble to the bedroom. His eyes are wide open. He smiles his little smile when he sees me. The first smile all weekend. I curl up with him and kiss him. He kisses back.

"You must be very tired," I say.

"Yes," he whispers.

"Do you want me to stay with you for a while?"

"Yes."

The Fat Lady Sings

"Would you like some more kisses?"

"Yes."

I kiss him until his eyes close again, and he drifts off to sleep. I lie beside him until I hear Carlotta's soft knock at the door.

The bed is delivered early in the morning. Lucy, Frenchie, and Hoo Hoo come down to help me lift him and do the morning tasks. His breathing has gotten worse. When Paul drops by, I ask about it. Is there anything we can do?

"No, David," he says. "Zero's just getting ready to die."

He slips in and out of consciousness. Begins to refuse food, drink, and medications. It's as though he's decided that enough is enough. As though he knows that if it's going to stop, he's the one who has to stop it. He seems unable to speak now, but his eyes remain bright and alert. He still squeezes back when I hold his hand.

There are still the routines of dressing, and diaper changes, keeping his mouth and eyes moist, the constant lifting and rolling to relieve the sores.

Friday dawns bright. Zero's breathing has a deep rattle. Carlotta calls in ill. She has pneumonia. I don't try to find a substitute. I just want to be alone here with him today.

We've set the hospital bed in the living room, so he faces out onto the garden. I unplug the phone. I hold his hand and talk to him through the morning and the afternoon. I change him, cleaning the dressings as needed. His breath thickens.

Hoo Hoo stops by on the way to a family reunion in British Columbia. She's headed for the airport. She gives him a quick hug before struggling down the steps to the waiting cab.

As evening falls, I am suddenly so exhausted I cannot keep my eyes open. I plug the phone in and call upstairs. Lucy comes right away. She makes me lie down and goes to sit with Zero. It seems I have just closed my eyes when she appears at my bedroom door.

"I think you better come," she says.

He's going, just as I reach the living room. His eyes are wide open and his head rolls toward me as I kneel beside him. His last breath escapes him like a sigh. I kiss his mouth, his face. "My darling, my sweet, sweet Zero," I cry. I hold him tightly against me. Then he's gone. Easy.

We close his eyes and lie him flat. His face has already set in a little smile. He looks pleased with himself. I kiss him again and again and again.

Lucy and I begin to call our friends. Our family. Within a half hour people begin to arrive. I reach Paul Cotes on his car phone. He's out in the suburbs somewhere.

"I'll be about four hours," he cautions.

"There's no rush."

Edie isn't in, but I catch Doll at home. Maybe it will be easier for Edie to hear it from her.

Edie calls back shortly. She's very cool and controlled. She thanks me again for the care I've taken of Zero. Then she asks me when she'll get her ashes. I can't deal with this.

"We'll talk later," I say.

"Fine," she snaps, slamming down the receiver.

Lucy and I eventually speak to, or leave messages for, everyone we know. From coast to coast.

The front room is full. People spill out over the deck into the garden. Cut flowers crowd the table. There's lots of food. And drink.

The Fat Lady Sings

As our friends arrive, I lead them in to the living room. I want them to see him. To touch him. To say good-bye if they can.

Millie staggers down, clutching a huge bottle of scotch. In all her years she's never seen a dead body. She wants Zero's face covered. Someone obliges. It is very wrong. I need to see him. I pull the sheet back down. We set Millie's chair around the corner, so she can't see him.

I am calm. Numb, perhaps, but it feels like calm.

I put on some show music. This is the last act of the musical comedy he and I so often joked that we were living. When "Hello Dolly" comes on, everybody sings. Searcy and Snookums lead a brief impromptu kick line.

Randy's mom, Dorothy, asks, "Do you guys dance at everybody's funeral?"

"Only if they deserve it, precious, only if they deserve it," gasps Snookums, collapsing out of breath on the couch.

There's lots of laughter, lots of tears.

Near midnight, Paul arrives. He's been stuck in traffic for hours on the 401. He signs the papers.

"You look absolutely exhausted," I say.

"Yeah, they're dying like flies out there," he replies, with a wan smile.

"Thanks for seeing us through to the end of this, Paul."

"It was a privilege," he says.

Paul's departure triggers an exodus. Before she leaves, Millie goes to Zero. She takes his face in her hands and says her farewell.

Finally, only Snookums, Searcy, Frenchie, and Lucy remain. We dress Zero in a soft plaid cotton shirt, bright with the colors he loved, yellow, purple, warm red, and forest green, fresh blue jeans, white socks.

"How are you, precious?" asks Snookums.

LABOUR OF LOVE

"Incredibly tired, incredibly calm, incredibly glad that he made it through."

"Well, this is how he always wanted to go, hon," adds Searcy, "here, at home, with you."

I look around at these, my dearest friends. "I'm so happy that I was able to get enough of my own health back, to see him to the end. What a gift." Suddenly, I feel like my heart has been torn out. The tears begin to well and spill down my cheeks.

"Come here, sweetie," says Searcy, pulling me into the crook of his arm, so my head rests on his shoulder. "You know, through all the years I knew Zero, it always seemed he was out there in life, performing on a tightrope. He always had been. And he continued right to the end, because he knew that you were always there to catch him should he fall.

"Now, he's off dancing in the stars, and for you the hard stuff just begins. But the rest of us are never far away, little darlin'. And don't you ever forget that."

We gather around the bed. Searcy begins to sing "The Rose," his old signature tune, from the grand old days of Show Babies, the bar, since demolished, where he first established himself as the reigning diva of Toronto. We sing along. Spontaneously, we each pick a song, as our good-bye. We sing our quavering solos, muff the words, harmonize, clutch each other as we laugh. And as we cry.

Finally, Frenchie says, "I don't know why, but I want to sing him the one that goes, 'I'll be down to get you in a taxi, honey, better be ready, by half-past eight . . .'"

"Oh! 'The Dark Town Strutters' Ball,'" I exclaim. "When we first met, I used to play him that on tissue paper and a comb. Wait a minute." I find a rolling paper in Zero's pot box, pull out my comb and give Frenchie the lead-in. We sing this one at the top of our lungs, till with a last flatulent blast from comb and paper, we dissolve into helpless laughter.

"Well, kids," I say, "this has been a long, long day."

The Fat Lady Sings

"Yeah," says Searcy, "we should go. Do you want one of us to stay, so you won't be alone?"

"No, Searcy, but thanks. I won't be alone."

When they're gone, I sit a moment, then call The Easy Way Out. We both made arrangements with them awhile back. They take care of everything: pick you up, file the paperwork, take you to the crematorium. The sincere man on the other end of the line asks when I'd like Mr. MacNoo's body to be picked up.

"About half-past eight," I reply with a giggle.

I strip to my shorts, climb into the hospital bed, and press myself against him. I can still feel his warmth through his clothes. I cradle him in my arms, and slip into instant, deep, and dreamless sleep.

The red finches are singing their hearts out on the deck when the somber young men arrive to take Zero away. Lucky man, to leave on the wings of so much song. The attendants are quick, efficient. I blow him one last kiss as they carry him down the steps. When I close the door behind them, the finches have stopped singing. It is unbearably still. My heart cracks in my chest.

The phone starts ringing at nine. It never stops. The reign of terror begins.

It is two days since Zero died.

"Searcy, I just do not know what to do. Edie has been calling me night and day."

"Whatever for?" he queries.

"Ashes! She's mad to get him into the ground down there. She's apparently planned a church service, the works. Everything Zero abhorred."

"I know, he hated all that stuff," Searcy agrees.

"She is consistent. She never listened to him when he was alive, so I guess it's too much to expect her to listen to him now that he's dead."

"What a nuisance," he commiserates.

"I only wish she'd back off and give me a moment to think this through."

"Not her style, sweetie."

"I was quite willing," I tell him, "to send or even deliver some of his ashes to her. Now, I don't know. I had a kind of spiritual journey mapped out in my mind. I'd scatter some of his ashes in San Francisco, New York, Saskatchewan, and here. I had also included Arkansas, but now I really don't know if I want that woman to get her hands on any part of him. Especially against his wishes. Seems like real bad karma. Bad voodoo."

"Have you even picked up the ashes yet?"

"No. The Necropolis called. They won't be ready until tomorrow noon."

"Okay, tomorrow let's have breakfast, then drive over and get them."

"You're a doll, Searce!"

"Yes, I am."

Doll calls. "David, I need you to do me a favor."

"What is it?"

"Please get those ashes down here."

"Doll, he just died. I only picked up the ashes today. I'll get ashes to you in my own good time. But I refuse to be bullied about it. What is it with you people, anyway?"

"Oh, you just don't understand. Mom has everything arranged for Zero's funeral. Invitations have been sent, the caterer has been contracted, the relatives are coming in from across the South. She and Sparky have even booked a combo for luncheon afterward by the swimming pool at Mom's condo."

The Fat Lady Sings

"This sounds like a dry run for your damned wedding. Doll, you know Zero did not want a funeral," I protest.

"Well, we do, and you've been driving Mom crazy, holding things up when she's gone to so much trouble. You could be more considerate."

"Yeah, I guess I could," I concede through gritted teeth. "Gotta go now."

I go into the living room and build a small fire in the fireplace. The first of the fall. I contemplate a course of action. When the embers have died down and cooled, I scoop some of the warm ash into a Zip-Loc bag. The ash is light and fine. I've decided that if Edie wants ashes, I'll give her goddamned ashes.

Searcy finds me hunched over the kitchen table, busy at my preparations. I have my mortar and pestle out and I'm grinding some blood and bone meal into a gritty powder.

"What in the world are you doing?"

"Preparing some ashes for Miz Edie, to get her off my back once and for all."

Searcy hoots. "Great idea, hon. I wondered when you were going to start fighting back. Zero would have approved. And she'll never know the difference."

"That's what I thought." I pour the powder in with the wood ash and mix them well. "There, that's better. I think this will do the trick very well."

Searcy rubs some of the ash between his thumb and forefinger. "Yeah, that feels quite authentic. There's not much here, though."

"I never specified how much I'd send her."

"You are a baaaad guy, David McLure!"

"Uh-huh," I nod with a smile. "And I could get worse. Much worse!"

LABOUR OF LOVE

We spend the afternoon shopping for a container for my handiwork. Finally in a mineral shop we find a perfect little onyx box.

Back at the house, I pop the "ashes" in the box and crazy-glue the lid shut. "Now," I ask, "what do I do?"

Searcy shrugs. "I don't know. I've never had to transport ashes across an international border before. Why don't you call the Necropolis? They must deal with these kinds of situations all the time."

"Good idea." I search out the number. A sexy-voiced young man answers. He sounds full of concern. I outline my dilemma.

"You know," he says, "I could send it for you, but all you need to do is bundle it up yourself and send it Priority Post. If you brought it here, I'd have to charge you one hundred dollars, and then I'd just go mail it Priority Post, anyway.

"And don't take it to the substation at Novak's Pharmacy. I tried to mail a friend there last week and they don't like to deal with the dead. Take it up to the big station on Charles Street."

"You've been a great help. What's your name?" I ask.

"Bradley."

"Well, thanks so much, Bradley."

"No problem, it's the least I can do. If we don't take care of each other, nobody else will."

I am already exhausted, so I decide to put off the post office until morning. The "ashes" will keep. Searcy bustles off to rehearsal and I stretch out on the couch. I'm asleep instantly. I wake up about four A.M., fully dressed, all the lights on, feeling terrible. I cannot get back to sleep.

About six A.M., the *Star* comes hurtling through the door. The headline reads: CANADA POST CALLS NATIONAL WALK-OUT. Shit! So now what do I do? They're predicting a long strike. Damn, damn, double damn, triple damn, hell! I wanted this to be over and done with. I want these crazy MacNoos off my back, so I can catch my breath, so I can think, and maybe even feel again. I'm dazed and exhausted.

The incessant phone calls demanding ashes have left me raw. Edie and Doll, a fiendish tag-team, seem to take turns leaving messages. They will not leave me be. I'm sick to death of hearing about their catering deadlines, and how Zero would have wanted this. I am buffeted by waves of grief, tension, and bone-deep fatigue. I feel my health begin to slip. The summer has caught up with me, and I'm in deep, deep trouble.

I answer the phone, hoping it will be the welcome voice of Searcy, or Snookums. No such luck. It's totally unfamiliar, portentious, and heavy with Arkansas twang. The voice identifies itself as Mr. Stonewall Boodie, Mortician, of Pine Bluff, Arkansas. Zero's hometown.

"Listen, son," Mr. Boodie intones, "I'm sorry to bother you, but we have a problem here."

"What's your problem, Mr. Boodie?" I ask.

"I need to have Mr. MacNoo's ashes here, pronto."

"I'll get them to you as fast as I can."

"Well, I need them now!" he says, with a rising note of desperation in his voice. "Miz MacNoo is being quite insistent. She is about to drive me and my staff right up the wall."

I outline my mailing dilemma to him.

"I really don't care!" he finally snaps. He's no longer polite. "Just get me some of the damned ashes! Miz MacNoo has been planning this event since July."

"July! He only died a few days ago!"

"Well, young feller, as you well know, Miz MacNoo believes in being prepared." His voice drops to a conspiratorial whisper, tinged with something that sounds like hysteria. "Listen, this woman is driving me crazy. She has everything booked for this weekend. If she don't have ashes by then, I don't know what she'll do."

"Something desperate, I presume. I just can't guarantee . . ."

"Just get me some of those damned ashes by the weekend, boy!" he growls. He hangs up.

I have had it! Zero died four days ago. I feel like I'm about to completely fall apart. I need to get this worked out.

I draw a tub of very hot water, add some bath oil, and climb in. As I sink into the heat, I start to shake. Tears spatter into the foam.

I hear the the deck door opening. "Are you in there? Are you all right?" It's Frenchie.

"Yeah, I'm in here. No, I'm not all right."

"Can I come in?"

"Yeah, sure." So much for a nice, quiet cry.

She swaggers in and peeks in the bathroom door. "Oooee! You're naked!" she exclaims. She parks herself on the edge of the tub.

"I find it the best way to bathe. You might want to try it sometime. Really revolutionary," I retort. "Sit down, why don't you?"

"Okay. Say, you don't look half bad . . . for a man."

"Thanks, pal."

"I've been worried about you. I haven't been able to catch you at home since Zero died. You'd better slow down, partner. It's time to take care of yourself."

I tell her the infernal saga of the ashes.

"Those bastards!" she growls. "How you gonna get her the goods?"

I shrug. "I'm tempted not to bother."

"Yeah, but you know she'll just stay on your back. It's like a Stephen King movie!" She ponders for a moment, idly doodling in the bubbles on my back and shoulders. I can see the wheels of her thought process in motion.

"Listen, David, do you have anything that you really have to be here for, for the next while?"

"Not really. There's the celebration for Zero, but that's three

The Fat Lady Sings

weeks away. And Snookums and Searcy seem to have it well in hand. Why?"

"Well, what say you get outa that tub, pack a little bag, and we hit the road for Arkansas? We could be there in a day and a half, two days, tops. We give Edie baby her damned ashes and it's over. You'll never have to deal with them again. Besides, honey, you really need to get out of town. What d'ya say?"

"A truly crazy, hare-brained idea! I like it!" I don't even really think about it. I leap up, dripping. "You're on, girlfriend!" I exclaim. I grab her in a wet, sudsy hug. "Let's blow this scene!" I've clearly lost my mind.

She seems very pleased with herself. She smacks me on the butt, then bustles up the stairs, checking her watch. "You've got half an hour, buddy, so move it," she calls out over her shoulder. "Oh, and you might want to put on some clothes. That getup is bound to arouse suspicion at the border."

I'm galvanized by the idea of getting away, of getting Edie out of my hair, of getting a grip on my tattered life. I throw some clothes into my sports bag. Dump in all my medications. I guess I'll tell the U.S. authorities they're vitamins, if they ask. I tuck the onyx box among my shorts.

I call Snookums at work. I tell him this latest lunatic plan. "Will you and Searcy ride herd on everything?"

"Of course, precious. Just don't wear yourself out, and don't fret. Everything will get looked after. Blaine's already picked up the case of Veuve Cliquot for Zero's party. Lots of folks have agreed to cook. It's going to be an amazing party. Oh, and did you mail the invitations?"

"The invitations! I'd forgotten." The day after Zero died, I had been looking for a photo of him to send to our friends with a death notice. I found the perfect shot. It's at Baker Beach, beneath the Golden Gate Bridge in San Francisco. Zero is leaping, naked, in the sunlight, extended in full flight. Gorgeous, smiling, flamboyant, he is suspended forever, flying and graceful in the sparkling air.

I had handwritten a message about his passing and invited our friends to join us to celebrate his life on Thanksgiving weekend a month away.

"Snookums, sweetie, you are a lifesaver! The invitations are here on the kitchen table. Millie came down yesterday and stamped them, but they do need to get mailed."

"Consider it done, precious. I'll pick them up this afternoon. Now, you have a good little journey and try to chill out. I hate to say this, David, but you're not looking at all well. I'll see you back here in a few days. If you run into any trouble call me. Anytime. And remember, precious, I love you very, very much."

He's choked me up. "Thanks, Snooks. Thanks for everything."

I leave a message for Searcy, then dial Lance's number. He's not in but his answering machine clicks on.

"Hey, darling, it's David. I'm headed for Little Rock this afternoon. We're driving and should be there in a couple of days. We won't be staying long, but is there any chance you and I can rendezvous, even for a hot moment? I'm aching to see you. I'll be in touch with Stellrita. Maybe she'd even let me bunk there. Anyway, she'll know where I am. Sure hope to see you. I love you very much."

I do love him. These past months of pouring everything into Zero, keeping him alive, keeping myself in constant, desperate motion, have limited us to phone calls and letters. All the frustrations that come of being far, far apart.

He kept wanting to come up and help. But since he had been ordered out of Canada only months before, I wouldn't let him. I told him to wait. Why risk queering a real solution to our immigration dilemma, if we're serious about being together? Yet, how I wanted him to be here. We had to find some way of getting him here with me on a permanent basis. Now, maybe, we can concentrate on that. If he still wants to.

The Fat Lady Sings

Frenchie breaks my reverie. She pokes her head in the door. "Are you about ready? We should hit the road."

I grab my sports bag and head for the door. I run back in and grab the green velvet bag containing the real Zero. What the hell! He might as well come along for the ride.

Frenchie is still in her crisp fortrel, orange and brown Zipolator uniform. I head for her lime-green, four-wheel-drive, all-terrain vehicle.

"No, pal, let's take the Zippo van. That way we have somewhere to sleep."

"Is that a good idea?" I ask.

"Yeah, I left a message with Vargas at the office. She'll cover for me. Anyway, I figure we'll be back by Monday."

I look at her skeptically.

She slings my bag into the back of the van. "Trust me, sport. Now, let's hit the road!"

VARMINTS!

We speed through the harvest-time abundance of Southern Ontario. Frenchie is a deft driver, but she drives very fast. I don't drive. Never have. I sit white-knuckled wondering why I've let this loon talk me into this excursion. At several points, I'm tempted to leap out when she slows momentarily at stop signs, but remember that this woman is a pro. She's fond of boasting of her fifteen accident-free years as Zipolator's top courier.

At the border she jokes with the U.S. officials, tips her hat jauntily, and speeds off. It's the first time in years that I haven't been hassled by U.S. Immigration. They always want to know what I do, where I work. They're usually fascinated by the stamps in my passport, Nicaragua, El Salvador, Grenada, scenes of so many recent triumphs for the American way. This time they ignore me. I'm slightly miffed. It must be because I don't look very dangerous these days.

We zip through the Michigan countryside. At this rate we'll be in Little Rock for supper. Frenchie is intent on the road. She hasn't spoken since the border. Once in a while she warbles along with the radio. We grab a bite at a little roadside hoagy stand.

The food doesn't sit well. I'm very, very tired. Suddenly I'm burning with fever. I slip into a fretful sleep. A particularly rough

113

stretch of pavement jars me into consciousness. I'm disoriented and soaked with sweat.

It's close to midnight. Suddenly Frenchie wheels into a little parking lot. A flickering neon sign identifies this place as Newt's Auto Wrecking and Salvage.

"Well, buddy, why don't you stretch out in the back and grab some shut-eye? Newt's an old throb from the sixties. I'm going to check her out. See if she remembers. Okay?"

I clamber into the back. She's thoughtfully laid out an air mattress and sleeping bag. I strip and crawl in. I'm dead tired.

The air is sweet and hot, full of the deep-bottomed rhythms of bull frogs in heat. Newt's seems to be located on the edge of a swamp. Lord know's where we are. I tumble quickly into sleep.

Stellrita sits on the cooler that Frenchie filled with sandwiches and beer at our last stop. I haven't seen her since the night I met Lance, since the MacNoo Family Capital Hotel Shoot-Out. She leans over, peering into my face.

"Davie, listen to me and listen good. Why would you be bringing that Zero boy's ashes back to Arkansas?" she growls. "Zero spent his entire life puttin' distance between himself and this damned place. He loved it and he hated it, but he did not ever want to be here. Do what you always meant to do, take his ashes to the places he loved—San Francisco, Saskatchewanee, New York City. You understand what I'm saying?" She squints at me hard, takes a deep draw on her cigarette, and then she's gone. I curl up and slip further into sleep.

Near dawn Frenchie wakens me as she creeps into the van. She's an absolute fright. Her hair stands on end and she has a cocky, shit-eating grin plastered all over her face. This cat has definitely swallowed the canary.

I sit up. "I assume old Newt was in," I say.

"Was she ever!" Frenchie crows. "That's one wild old broad and boy, was she glad to see me. And that gal has gotta be seventy if she's a day. Like a fine wine, she's only improved with age." Frenchie checks herself out in the mirror. "But then so have I." She spits on her fingers and tries to pat down her crazy hair.

She gives me a minute to scramble into my clothes, then throws the van into reverse. We hit the highway in a hail of flying gravel.

We stop briefly and wolf down huge greasy plates of bacon and eggs. Frenchie is talking today. Stream of consciousness. Hardly stopping for breath. I'm silent.

About noon I begin to feel like shit again. Alternately burning hot, then freezing cold. Fever and chills. I climb into the back and lie down. Frenchie pulls over to the side of the road.

"You okay?" she asks.

"No."

"Wanna go back"

"Why bother?" I reply through chattering teeth. "Let's get this circus back on the road."

She looks at me nervously. "You're the boss, pal, but you sure don't look so hot."

I curl up again and try to sleep it through. I feel delirious. Stellrita fades in and out of my head. Today she's not saying anything but she still peers intently into my face as though she's searching for something. Every once in a while she nods as though she's found it.

I'm semi-comatose. Not asleep, not awake. Sweating, shivering, burning. Frenchie is constantly checking me out in the rearview mirror. She's clearly worried. She's slowed down to something near the speed limit. Suddenly she jams on the brakes.

"My period!" she exclaims. "It must be goddamned menopause. My fuckin' period has started again and I only finished one six days ago. Really, there should really be a law exempting lesbians from this kind of nonsense.

"Listen, David, I've got to get me some pads. Then I'm gonna find us a motel and maybe a doctor. You're looking worse all the time."

LABOUR OF LOVE

I just stare at her. My head is on fire. I give her what I think is a cheery smile. "It could be worse," I point out.

"Yeah, you could be dead! And really, pal, if we're late for Edie's event, she can just sit on it till we get there. We're not gonna kill you just because she's got her caterers booked.

"I don't even really know where the hell we are," she grumps. "You haven't been a very good navigator lately. We're crossing a big bridge right now, but I didn't even notice what the sign said. There're lights, though, ahead on the other side."

What seems like mere minutes later she exclaims, "It's a little Piggly Wiggly store. They must have tampons." She hops out of the van. "I'll be back in a minute, then I'm gettin' you to bed somewhere. Okay, pal?"

Stellrita looms in my face again. "Take a message from the Mud Folk. The Mississippi Mud Folk," she rasps.

In my haze, I vaguely remember a tale she'd told Zero, years ago, about the Mud Folk, a band of the dispossessed who live on the mud flats on the Arkansas side of the Mississippi. She told him then, that if he ever needed help, to go to them. Told him to tell them Stellrita sent him.

"Where are they?" I ask.

"Nearby."

I get up on my knees. I'm suddenly very dizzy. Every inch of my skin aches. I grab my bag, open the back door of the van and tumble out onto my shoulder. Pain knifes through me. The air is thick and swampy, full of the sounds of frogs and night birds.

I stagger to my feet and head into the darkness. I think I hear Frenchie call my name. I turn to respond, lose my footing and crash down a steep incline, coming to rest at last in a tall dense canebrake at the bottom. I'm lying in several inches of water. I'm wet and sore and exhausted. I can't move.

Frenchie is thrashing about in the weeds somewhere in the

116

Varmints!

darkness above me. She keeps calling my name, a rising note of panic in her voice.

"Damn it, David. Where are you? We're almost there. We're already on the Arkansas side of the Mississippi. Now you just come on out. This has gone on long enough." She makes it sound like I'm a recalcitrant child, too zealous at a game of hide-and-seek.

I try to call out. Can't make my voice work.

She's quiet for a moment, then mutters "Gotta get help." I hear the van door open and close. She revs the engine.

A screen door slams nearby. A woman's voice thick with Arkansas twang shouts, "You best pipe down out here, honey. People are trying to sleep."

Frenchie apologizes for the noise and explains that she's lost me.

"I bet your friend has just hitched his way on into Little Rock. I'm sure nobody stole him. The State Police are just up the highway a piece. You want me to call them?"

"I think I'll just drive up a ways," says Frenchie, "and see if my pal is on the road. I can stop at the trooper station if I don't sight him. But thanks. And if my friend appears make him lie down and wait. He was looking real sick."

"Well, sure, honey," the woman replies. "I'll check around here a bit and you see if he's on the highway."

I hear Frenchie drive away. I'm sure she'll be back in a moment with help. She isn't, though. I pull myself to my feet. I try to climb back up the bank. I can't make it. I just keep sliding further down in the weeds. I lie there muddy and exhausted. Suddenly, a flashlight shines directly in my eyes. I peer up into a round, sunburned face.

"Laws sake, young feller, you are a sorry sight if I ever did see one. Here, let me help you up outa that swamp." She clambers down the embankment and hoists me to my feet. Then slipping and stumbling, she half-drags me back up to the road.

LABOUR OF LOVE

"Honey, you are on fire!" she exclaims. "I'm gonna get you into bed right this minute!"

My knees begin to buckle. My head reels. The flickering light above the door we're headed for barely illuminates a crudely lettered sign that proclaims PIGGLY WIGGLY STORE/MUD FOLK MOTEL/SPACE RESEARCH AND GIZMOS, CHARLES MACNOO & PATTI CAKE, PROPRIETORS. EVERYBODY WELCOME!

I wake with a start. I have no idea where I am. I'm stretched out on a huge, battered sofa in a strange room. Zero's dad is sitting by my side. He snaps to attention when he sees my eyes open. He leaps to his feet and salutes, then reaches out to pump my hand enthusiastically.

"Mighty glad you dropped by, young feller. The Almighty Goddess had mentioned in a recent dispatch that we might expect a visitation."

"Charles, I don't know if you remember me," I say cautiously. "I'm David McLure, Zero's friend."

He looks at me as though I'm seriously deranged. "Of course I know you!" he protests. "I have long been in close personal contact with many of you northern aliens."

He's wearing silver-gray polyester pants with white fur cuffs. They're short in the leg and belted high. His huge belt buckle proclaims "Space Cadet." A red and yellow embroidered vest covers a faded purple jersey. On the back of his vest orange felt letters have been glued haphazardly to declare "Raized by wolves." He has a tattoo of a space invader on his left arm. Silver and turquoise bangles rattle on his arm and an eagle-feather medallion hangs around his neck. He looms over me, still standing at attention.

"At ease, Charles," I order.

He relaxes. Switches gears. "Are you all right, David?" he asks, full of concern. "You've been raving delirious all night." He places his big warm hand on my forehead. "I think maybe your fever's broken. We've been mighty worried. You still look real peaked."

"What about Frenchie? Did she come back?" I ask.

"Frenchie?" he looks perplexed. "Oh, your friend. I called the state troopers and they caught up to her a little ways up the road. She was kind of frantic. I told her we'd found you and for her to go on into Little Rock. Said we'd send you in as soon as your fever went down. So she's holed up at Stellrita's, waitin' to hear from you. She's been callin'."

"Thanks, Charles."

I hear the sound of eggs being cracked and bacon beginning to fry. I'm suddenly dizzy with hunger.

A woman enters carrying thick mugs of rich, steaming coffee. She looks at me intently from under the brim of her hat. They are both wearing Razorback hog hats. She's wearing a T-shirt that across her chest promises the best burger at Say Macintosh's Famous Little Rock Restaurant. Across her belly is a picture of a black man punching a jowly old white guy in the head. I recognize the image immediately. I have the same one taped to my fridge door.

Say Macintosh, Little Rock's self-styled "Black Santa Claus," is famous throughout Arkansas as a restaurateur, philanthropist, and tireless fighter for the rights of the downtrodden. Some think he's just a shameless publicity hound. Anyway, the image on her T-shirt had appeared, even in the Toronto newspapers, earlier this year when Say had whacked a member of the Ku Klux Klan, his opponent for some local civic office.

Charles announces, "This here is my beloved new wife, sidekick, confidante, and business partner, Miz Patti Cake!" He sounds like a game show host.

She grimaces at me, puts down the coffee, and takes my hand in a powerful grip. "Well, you look a dang-sight better than you did last night. It's a pleasure to meet you."

119

"Thanks for dragging me out of the ditch. I'd probably have died there."

"It was nuthin'," she snorts. "I would have done it for a dog."

She heads back into the next room. There is some spirited clattering then she barks, "Y'all come on in here now. Don't let this food get cold."

Charles helps me to my feet and steers me into the kitchen. It's a sun-filled place with a small counter and one booth. Patti has set out three huge plates of bacon, eggs, and hot biscuits with gravy. We dig in.

"I am so hungry," I announce, "and this food is so good."

She reaches out and pats my hand. "Y'all better slow down, boy, or you're going to founder."

"So, Charles, are you going to this funeral Edie's been planning for Zero?" I ask.

"No, I've got a lot of stuff to do here. I think it best I remember him in my own manner," he responds.

"Truth is," growls Patti, "he wasn't even asked. We only found out about it through Stellrita. I tell you, if that Edie MacNoo ever crosses my path on this earth I fully intend to snatch her bald!"

She gives me that crooked grimace again, which I've finally figured out is her smile.

"I'd give my eyeteeth to witness that encounter," I chuckle. I like this Patti Cake.

"How did you two meet?" I ask.

"We was both in the same manic-depressive support group. I run short of Lithium and Charles borrowed me some of his. One thing led to another. You know how that is." She twists her face at me again and makes the startled choking sound, which for her is laughter. She's warming to me.

Charles chimes in. "We haven't really gotten married. We've been too busy havin' a great time, I guess. We heard about this place being' for sale, so Patti sold her little house in North Little Rock and quit her checkout job at the Wal-Mart."

"After twenty-three years," she says with a mixture of pride and relief. "And here we are just havin' a whale of a time."

"It helps that we're both nuttier than fruitcakes!" Charles hoots. He pushes back from the table. "Now, I suppose we should get you on the road to Little Rock, if you're going to get those ashes to her high and mightiness, Miz Edie."

"Yeah, I guess so." I'm reluctant to leave this sun-drenched room and this crazed but happy pair.

Charles has arranged a ride to Little Rock for me with the motel's only other guest. A horn toots in the yard. We head out the screen door.

A great, blond giant smiles lazily from behind the steering wheel of a small pink school bus. On the side of the bus, it says, "The Happy Little Sunday School Bus. Church of the Holy Magic." A huge, grinning mouth has been painted in the front, incorporating the grillwork as teeth. Perpetually amazed eyebrows have been drawn above the headlights. The intent seems to be to create a cheerful, storybook image of a friendly bus, smiling and busy at its tasks. Unfortunately, the elements combine instead to give it the look of a drunkenly leering, mechanical carnivore, hungry for roadkill.

"This here is Auto," says Charles. Auto reaches across the bus and shakes my hand. He is a monster.

Charles says, "David, I want you to know how much I appreciate you. I know that losing him must be hard. It's damned hard for me. He was my special child. But you were his special friend. You took real good care of him. I know that and I thank you." He salutes me smartly. There are tears in his eyes.

Patti punches me lightly on the shoulder. "You're always welcome here, David. Remember that. I never met Zero, but I've heard some of the tales. You're a good man." She snaps me a salute as well.

LABOUR OF LOVE

"Thank you, Patti. You two take real good care of each other, okay?" I climb into the bus.

"Now, Auto," Patti calls, "there is fried chicken, biscuits and gravy in that there paper sack I gave you. See that David gets some of it."

"And take him right to Stellrita's. He's a man with a mission," orders Charles.

"Y'all don't be a stranger," Patti croaks as the bus door closes behind me.

When I look back to wave to them, they are saluting again, standing shoulder to shoulder. They look like veterans of some wacky war. And I guess they are. Mud Folk.

Auto doesn't say much. He does smile a lot. I still feel wrung out. Unsteady.

What the hell am I doing here, sick as a dog, motoring through Arkansas with a beautiful blond giant in a pink Sunday School bus, to deliver fake ashes to people I have come to despise? None of it makes sense. Not at this point. Maybe never.

I sneak a glance at Auto's vast blondness. "When do you think we'll get there?" I inquire.

"Shortly." He grins and reaches over and gives my thigh a comradely squeeze. Or is it? Whoa now! I think I've got enough on my plate as it is. Yet the instant surge of blood to my cock is a welcome reassurance.

A half hour later Auto shakes me awake. We are parked outside of the sprawling house where Stellrita lives, where Zero grew up. Zero's grandfather, Walter Jackson MacNoo, bequeathed this place to her. She lives here now with her daughter, Helen Howard, the child she bore him.

I can see Stellrita crouched in her rocker on the porch. I swear she hasn't moved since I last saw her there.

I haul my bag down the bus steps.

"Can I help you?" asks Auto.

Varmints!

"No, it's okay. Thanks a million for the ride." I reach up and shake his giant hand. The sun gilds the white-blond hair on his freckled forearm. Mmmm. Luscious. There's life in the old girl yet!

"Hope y'all have a good time." He gives me a big lazy smile. "Maybe we'll cross paths while you're here."

I'm still weak. Even the short ride into Little Rock has tired me. I trudge up the sidewalk staggering a bit with the bag. Stellrita's head snaps up when she hears me dragging my feet on the walk as I cross the yard.

"Who goes there?" she demands, shading her eyes to peer out of the cool shadows of the porch.

"David, Zero's friend from Canada," I reply.

"I know you, don't I? Ain't you the fellah from Saskatchewanee?" she asks.

How does she know that? "Yes, I am."

"Well, we'll talk about that later. Right now we gotta get our tired butts over to Edie's spectacle. Park your bag over here beside me. We'll head on over there as soon as that gal Frenchie returns from delivering the ashes."

"What ashes? I've got all the ashes here with me."

"Figured as much," she says, "but you weren't here, were you? You was off hobnobbin' with the Mud Folk. Meanwhile, old Edie was in a frenzy. We couldn't let the poor soul down."

"But . . ."

"Yo, buddy!" I hear Frenchie's familiar voice as she jumps out of the van and struts across the yard. She runs the last ten yards. Hugs me very hard. "You scared the hell out of me, you little shit!" she shouts.

"Scared the hell out of myself," I reply.

"Are you okay?" she asks, her voice soft with tender concern.

"Tired and a mess, but still alive." I smile.

She's wearing her brown and orange fortrel Zipolator delivery uniform. She looks like she's having the time of her life.

LABOUR OF LOVE

"This Stellrita is one hot babe," she proclaims.

Stellrita chuckles. "And don't you ever forget it, toots," she growls from her shaded perch. "Now, help me up, and let's get over to that boneyard and check out the action. How did the delivery go?"

"Smooth. A piece o' cake," says Frenchie, obviously pleased with herself.

"Didn't they recognize you?" I can't wait to find out what these two have been up to.

"Hell, no. I'm simply another peon in a uniform. Edie treated me just like she did when she was in Toronto. Looked right through me. Like I wasn't even there. She wouldn't know me if I was floating in her soup." She chuckles. "I did get a nice fat tip out of Sparky, though."

We bundle into the Zipolator van. Frenchie has apparently used her short time in Little Rock to full advantage. She already seems to know the city. What a pro!

We roar up to the cemetery. Frenchie guns the motor a couple of times before shutting off the engine. She's enjoying this.

A sign at the cemetery gates announces that the interment of the "cremains" of Zero MacNoo will occur at three o'clock in the family plot. It's three-ten. It looks like the "funeral" is about to begin. The assembled relatives are milling around what I assume is the family plot.

I recognize most of them from previous encounters. They're all here, from Dallas, Houston, Eldorado, Hot Springs, Bald Knob, and Memphis. Aunt Enid and Doc, Aunt Caroline and Uncle Will, Will looking, if possible, even more frail than when I last saw him, Aunt Lorna, Uncle John, and assorted cousins whose names I've never been able to retain. The "interment of the cremains" seems to have provided a prime shopping opportunity. As usual, all of the women are elegantly dressed. Some even in furs beneath the broiling sun.

Off to the side, Aunt Tula squats on a little camp stool. Her bulk virtually conceals the stool. She seems to be hovering in the air about a foot and a half above the ground.

People continue to appear. A flurry of air-kissing and crocodile tears greets each new arrival. Edie, in a barely controlled frenzy, as is her wont, is being brave on Sparky's arm.

Her favorite cousin, Farley Potts, a homosexual Episcopalian priest, waddles across the lawn. He mops at his brow with a large white monogrammed handkerchief. I only know him from photos, but recognize him at once.

Edie had always held him up to Zero as a role model of how the homosexual should be. As Zero said, "Comfortable, closeted, and a coward."

Stellrita parks herself beneath a tree at the entrance. Frenchie disappears.

I feel light-headed and queasy in the heat. "Listen," I mutter to no one in particular, "I don't want to talk to any of these people. I don't even want to be here." I skirt the gathering and sit on a cool headstone in the shade of a huge catalpa tree. There's a good view of the proceedings, and it's unlikely anyone will notice or recognize me in the flickering, sun-dappled shadows beneath the catalpa.

For the life of me, I have no idea what they're burying, since I have both my alternatives in my backpack. What they assume to be Zero sits on a small, gilded baroque stand which usually graces the front hallway of Edie's luxury condo. The "cremains" are in an ornate little chest centered on an elaborate lace doily. It looks like a box of bonbons on a bedside table. Except, it's draped in one of those ubiquitous U.S. flags waved with such vigor by the American populace at public events. Beside the table is a large headstone topped with a cross. I can't read the inscription from my vantage point. I don't want to. A little mound of fresh earth designates the final resting spot for the "cremains." It looks like a gopher hole. Large pots of rapidly wilting mums are everywhere.

LABOUR OF LOVE

Farley gives his face another swab, then begins his eulogy.

This is a fantasy construction of Zero's life in which Zero becomes the dutiful, doting, and successful son Edie had always hoped for. A livelier version of his lumpish elder brother Norm. Farley does manage to slip in Zero's gayness, a condition he describes as "an affliction." He notes, however, that he bore this particular burden well. There's no mention of friends or relationships. To the unaware, Zero is portrayed as a dull, blissful ninny, sustained exclusively in the bosom of his beloved family.

"Bullshit, bullshit, bullshit!" Frenchie mutters at my elbow, where she's suddenly appeared. "I thought Zero left specific instructions about not wanting any of this phony bullshit."

"It's true, but since they never respected his choices when he was alive I hardly expect them to respect them when he's dead."

"Bastids!" she growls.

Farley, clearly enamored with his own plummy tones, is really wound up. People begin to shuffle and surreptitiously check their watches. The sun has already passed the yardarm and they are ready for their afternoon cocktails. It's broiling hot out here, and these razorbacks are eager to get to the trough.

Edie begins to make hand signals to gain Farley's attention. He, however, is busy elaborating a metaphor about Zero as an electric light bulb. Her gestures become increasingly agitated, until he can no longer safely ignore them. She makes a throat-cutting motion. He makes an exaggerated little moue with his mouth, but winds down quickly. Episcopalian incantations of some sort are then directed at the "cremains."

Aunt Tula, who is nearly completely deaf, tugs at her daughter Lorna's sleeve and demands in a loud voice, "Isn't that a damned small box for that boy? I always remember him as being bigger. And what the sam hell are these 'cremains' that fat dope Farley keeps going on about? When can we get out of here? I'm hungry!"

Edie glares at Aunt Tula, then turns to Sparky and snarls, sotto

Varmints!

voce, "Tula is a nuisance and a burden to all around her. Why should we lose my Zero and not that mean old woman? There is no justice."

"Y'all sure better hope there isn't, Miz Fancy Pants," bellows Aunt Tula. "I hear a lot more than you think I do. Lorna, help me to my feet. I want to go."

"We'll be going as soon as Bitsy sings, Mother. Now please hush," Lorna pleads.

A woman in a flaming-red, full-length dress steps shakily forward. I recognize her. Her name is Bitsy something or other. Zero and I joined Edie and her at The Little Rock Club for afternoon drinks several years ago. She looks like Carol Channing, but thinner. It seems Bitsy's going to wind things up with a song.

Her high heel catches in the turf and she pitches forward. The heel snaps off. Her dentures pop out of her mouth and go hurtling through the air. A mangy yellow dog that has been lying on its side panting in the sizzling heat is galvanized by this turn of events. Before anyone can respond, the hound leaps into the air, fields the flying teeth out of the air, and hightails it out of the graveyard.

People are trying to maintain some semblance of solemnity and decorum, but I know they must be peeing themselves. The dog is long gone and nobody makes any effort to pursue it. It's just too hot.

Without her teeth, Bitsy looks like a dried-apple doll. She's weeping, but is obviously a trooper. She limps to the front of the gathering. She kicks off her good shoe, then stands there blinking in the blazing sun. She shields her mouth with one hand and holds her shoe in the other.

In a high clear soprano, she begins to sing the interminable traditional folk song, "Barbara Allen." This selection seems to have no obvious connection to the proceedings, other than its relentless tragedy.

Bitsy performs well and her continuing freshets of tears lend a heartbreaking pathos, previously lacking, to the proceedings. Some seem moved, but the crowd is getting more restive. Farley cuts her off as she's about to launch into yet another plaintive verse and chorus.

He announces that cocktails and luncheon will be served poolside at Edie's condo. Hart Border and his combo will entertain. There is a palpable air of relief at this news.

"And it's about damned time, too," wheezes Aunt Tula, as she again attempts to heave herself up from her camp stool. Aunt Lorna helps her to her feet.

Zero's nephew and niece, Rotten Dog and Little Cookie, have been enthusiastically vandalizing the cemetery during the ceremony. Somehow they have managed to up-end a hideous angel and rush madly about informing everyone of their accomplishment.

Edie is supported on one side by Sparky and on the other by Farley. Farley is beaming. He's very pleased with his performance today.

There does seem to be some real grief. Doll weeps broken-heartedly. The stolid Harry Honeyfat, Junior, comforts with a sun-burned arm around her shoulder. Aunt Enid looks sorrowful and stricken. Some folks I've never met, probably old school friends, huddle together weeping quietly. Two young women in big flat identical blue hats cry in each other's arms. Some black women stand off to the back and sides. I recognize Lutherette. Lance's mother, Helen Howard, is here, as well.

Frenchie and I hang back to give the mourners time to disperse. I hear a burst of high-pitched laughter. Stellrita is doubled-up, leaning against a tree near the entrance. She's cackling so hard she can hardly stand. Tears roll down her wizened cheeks.

Edie spies her and quickens her pace. Stellrita, now prostrate by the side of the path, pounds the ground with her gnarled fists and howls with laughter.

The crowd slows as they skirt Stellrita warily. Edie smiles tightly. She's aghast at this development. Probably thinks Stellrita still has rabies.

Varmints!

"Well, Stellrita," she remarks, through a frozen smile, "I'm certainly moved that you share our grief."

"Don't share nobody's grief," Stellrita responds, gasping for breath from her prone position. "I have my own grief. Which is none of your biness, you meddlin' fool. 'Sides, I'm laughin', not cryin'!"

Edie is incensed. "This is not a time for levity, you crazy heathen woman! Have you no respect?"

"Got lots of damned respect," Stellrita replies. She's caught her breath, and aside from a periodic, asthmatic wheeze, speaks calmly. She shifts to a more comfortable position, but continues to gaze up at the sky. "There's just sumthin' 'bout all you high-toned hillbillies crying crocodile tears over Zero that tickles me. Y'all treat the boy like shit for most of his days on this earth, then once he dies y'all start wailin' and gnashin' your teeth. I do find that funny. I have seen this family up close now for most of my hundred and twenty-two years and y'all are still the same bunch of mean-spirited phonies you always been."

Edie looks on the verge of kicking her. Sparky and Farley tighten their grips on Edie's arms and start to gently herd her to the mortician's waiting limo.

She shouts, "I don't know why your family or the state officials haven't locked you up, you miserable crone. I'm going to get you put away, if it's the last thing I do!"

"Edie, darling," Sparky tries to reason with her, "you know that won't work. Remember when you set up that table at the mall last year, with the public petition to have her declared criminally insane? Well, honey, people thought that it was you that was crazy.

"She's just too much history on the hoof. Besides, she's been around so long she's got the goods on everybody."

"That's what I mean, she's a public menace!" Edie raves.

Stellrita looks at her. "He's right, Miz Edie. Don't push it. You don't really want to tangle with this old woman."

LABOUR OF LOVE

Then, with amazing speed, Stellrita rolls over onto her hands and knees. She scampers down the sidewalk toward Edie, barking and growling.

Edie looks horrified. It's her hydrophobic nightmare revisited. She sprints for the car, leaving her escorts puffing in her wake. She scrambles in and locks the door.

Stellrita has again dissolved into helpless laughter on the walk.

"Oo-ee! Did you see the speed on that woman?" She's still chuckling when she spies Bitsy trying to edge by her without being noticed. "Oh, by the way, Miz Bitsy, I done rescued yer teeth from that dawg." She brandishes the dentures at Bitsy.

Bitsy's face breaks into a smile behind her hand. Something has been salvaged. "Why, thank you, Stellrita, I surely do appreciate that," she mumbles from behind her hand.

"It was nothin', ma'am," Stellrita assures her. "I did have quite a tussle with the mutt, but he finally puked 'em up and I grabbed 'em. I think maybe they bit him back." This amuses her to no end and she howls with laughter again.

Bitsy looks horrified, but snatches the offered mouthful and hobbles across the hot pavement to her car. She's awash in a fresh torrent of tears.

Edie is just visible through the tinted glass of the limo. As the car pulls away she seems to be shouting and shaking her fist at Stellrita.

Smiling sweetly, Stellrita waves back.

The three of us are back on Stellrita's porch. The ice tea's been poured. I'm exhausted. Stellrita is in exuberant high spirits.

"Okay, you two, what the hell did those lunatics bury out there today?" I demand.

"Varmints!" hoots Stellrita.

"Varmints?"

Varmints!

"When Frenchie showed up here sayin' she'd lost you in a ditch somewhere and couldn't find any ashes in the van, we was wondering what we could provide so old Edie's cemetery cocktail hour could go on. We knew y'all was carrying ashes of some description, but after Charles called, we thought we could perhaps do you a favor."

"So we got creative!" crows Frenchie.

"Yes, sir. I took my gun and shot us a passel of those pesky tree rats out of that big pecan in the back. Me and Toots here skinned 'em and had us a big old squirrel pie."

"Then we just burned what was left of the little suckers in the barrel in the backyard," adds Frenchie.

"I had me an inlaid little box that Zero's granddaddy Walter Jackson MacNoo give me fifty, sixty years ago. We popped the varmint residue in that box and glued her shut. Frenchie put on her official delivery outfit and whipped 'em over to Mister Boodie, the mortician."

"And not a minute too soon," says Frenchie. "Edie was havin' a conniption fit, goin' up one side of that poor Boodie fellah, and down the other."

I shake my head. "Squirrels! I'm glad you too had such a good time."

"Least we could do," says Stellrita. "And hell, I haven't laughed so hard at a funeral since Zero's granddaddy died."

"What happened then?" asks Frenchie, eager for a tale.

"I remember it like it was only yesterday," Stellrita begins. She giggles at this. "'Course, in truth, these days I can't often actually remember yesterday!

"It was pretty much the same dang bunch of reprobates that was there today, give or take a few. They was all after Walter's money. Millin' around his bed. Jostlin' for position, hopin' to catch his eye. All dreamin' they was the big winner in his will. None of 'em could stand the old bugger and he felt the same way about them.

"Suddenly, Walter sat bolt upright and declared, 'I pledge allegiance to America.' He paused. 'I pledge allegiance to the United States of America.' He paused again. He had everybody's attention, since, at that point, he ain't said more than a few cuss words for days. 'What comes next?' he ask. 'What comes after I pledge allegiance to America?'

"Hortense says, 'I can't imagine.'

"Charles MacNoo says, 'I pledge allegiance to the flag of the United States of America.'

" 'Yes,' agrees Hortense, 'That's it.'

" 'But, after that?' asks Walter.

" 'To forgive our trespasses as those who trespass against us?' one of those Houston uncles says.

" 'That's the Lord's Prayer, for God's sake. Haven't you ever been in a church?' ask Edie. 'I pledge allegiance to the flag of the United States of America, and of . . ., no, and to, it's to.'

" 'To what?' asks Hortense.

" 'To the republic!' shout Lorna. It begins to sound like one of them game shows on the TV.

"At that point Walter says, 'The republic!' then lay back down.

" 'For which it stands, one nation under God. There's your God, Edie, with justice and liberty for all!' says Marcus.

" 'Liberty and justice,' Edie shoots back.

"Hortense replys, 'Liberty and justice? No, justice and liberty. I'm sure it's justice and liberty.'

"Lorna wades in again, 'It's not. It's liberty and justice.'

"Hortense is adamant. 'Justice and liberty! Liberty can not come before justice. Isn't that right, Walter? Walter!'

"Well, the old cuss expired while they was all trying to reconstruct the 'Pledge of Allegiance.' I already put pennies on his eyelids and was combin' his hair when they noticed he was gone.

"They was in such a flap. The look on those faces! I started to laugh. Well, I thought for sure I'd bust a gusset. Once they all realized he were dead and they hadn't got his will altered, they was mad as hornets. Child, you never heard such caterwaulin.' Shoutin' at each other, all red-faced and angry, accusin' each other of this and that. And I couldn't stop laughin'. Finally, I thought I'm gonna pee myself for sure. I headed down the hallway. I got to the back kitchen. And that's when I sat down and cried."

"Now, there's still some of that good old squirrel pie left. It's always better cold. How 'bout you go rustle that up for us, Frenchie? It's all in them covered dishes in the summer kitchen."

"Sure thing, boss woman," says Frenchie.

I move over to sit on the floor beside Stellrita. She puts her gnarled hand on my head.

"Well, David, you and me done lost one of the best. He was my all-time favorite. I sure do hope to see him again real soon. He's the only one I'd care to, him and my last husbin', Trombone."

"I'd love to see him again, too," I say, "but I could wait awhile."

A cloud passes over her face. "Your not doin' too well, your own self, are you, boy? I can only wish you well and I only hope you have someone to take as good care of you, as Frenchie tells me you took care of my Zero."

"No guarantees of that," I reply.

"Well, I know a fellah from here who'd sure like to," she says. "Young Lance has been pinin' for you sumthin' fierce. It's been hellish for the boy to be stuck down here when he wants to be up there with you."

"It's a lot to ask," I reply. "I don't know if it's fair to carry on with him when my own time is running out."

She knuckles my head. Hard. "Don't be stupid!" she snaps. "Nuthin' in this damn world is fair, mister, and you of all people should know that by now. Sure, it's a lot to ask, but you gain nuthin' by not askin'. He got the option to say yes or no. But you gotta respect his right to do that.

LABOUR OF LOVE

"He called this mornin' and he's takin' the bus up from New Orleans this evenin'. Y'all can stay here in the old slave shed in the back. I won't even charge you. For the first night anyway!"

It's late. Frenchie clears the dishes and heads for Discovery II to frolic with some local lesbians she met over ribs at Say Macintosh's. Helen's gone to bed. Stellrita and I sit out in the hot and humid air. We listen to the solitary calls of the nighthawks, the hypnotic, trilling chorus of the cricket frogs in the giant oak that shades the porch.

After a long while Stellrita says, "I believe Zero once told me y'all was from Saskatchewanee?"

"Yes ma'am. It's called Saskatchewan, though."

"That's what I said, Saskatchewanee," she snaps. "I bin there."

"You've been to Saskatchewan?" I am intrigued.

"Sure was. It were back near the turn of this century. I was grubbin' out an existence on a little piece of dirt over west of Blue Ball toward Pilot Knob. One day I looked up from the few measly ears of corn I was shuckin' into the face of the most beautiful man I have ever seen in my long and miserable life. Bar none. And I've seen me a few.

"He shook my hand and told me his name was Almighty Moose Nose.

"He were an Injun. Long black hair in braids. The works. I was a little frighted 'cause he'd sorta crept up on me, silentlike. But he smiled and I smiled. I offered him a dipper of cold water from the well. He asked if he could sit awhile. He spoke English pretty well, but different from folks around here. It turns out he was a horse trader peddlin' nags all over the West. He had a string of four or five with him. I told him to turn 'em loose in my pasture and I'd rustle him up some grub.

"Well, we hit it off dandy. One thing led to another and he lingered on with me for quite a spell. But then he got restless. One day he asked me if I would be his mate and go on with him up to the land of Saskatchewanee where he come from.

"Saskatchewanee. What did I know? I'd never heard of it before. I suspected it was probably just over the Oklahoma border a piece. I was barely scratchin' out enough food to live on that sorry piece of earth I'd squatted. And I had me a powerful urge for Mister Moose Nose, and he for me. There was no debate really.

"We lit out. Got carried away at a tent revival outside of Fort Smith and got some drunken, rantin' preacher to marry us. Don't know why we bothered since we was both heathens of some description. Anyway, I headed north as Missus Almighty Moose Nose.

"It were some journey. We traveled seemed like forever. North and north and north. I was havin' a hell of a time with Almighty and by the time I sobered up enough to panic, I was so far from where I come from I thought I might as well keep going.

"Well, we trekked on through that Big Sky country. Way up past the flat lands of the prairies. Deep in the bush in the northwest. This was Saskatchewanee, Almighty told me.

"We roamed around through those endless woods till we joined up with his peoples. They was good folks. Savages, to my mind. But then so was I, more or less. So was everybody in those days. It was not a peculiar condition.

"I spent two years and a bit in that place with him. We run a trap line along the Waterhen River. Had me a pretty little daughter, 'Meecheeswasis' in that Cree language, 'White Swallow' in English, but she died."

"It was too damned cold in the winter, too many bugs in the summer. I had big grief over that baby, and Almighty was wanderin'. And I missed this other godforsaken place, so I packed up one day when he was out tom-cattin' around, I took me a horse and lit out southward. Don't rightly know how I found my way back but I come home to Zero's grandaddy and several more husbins. I never bothered to divorce Almighty and he never came after me."

"Why, that was bigamy!" I say.

"You bet it was big of me!" She cackles with delight at the old joke until she's bent-over, wheezing. She regains her breath and takes a long, deep drag on her cigarette.

"Do you miss that cold country?" she asks.

"It's where I come from," I reply. "It's an important part of who I am, who I turned out to be."

She nods. "I understand that. Just like this miserable ignorant swamp is for me. You know, except for Saskatchewanee, I ain't never gone far. I always came back. Couldn't get away. I'm mighty glad that Zero got out, though. I wasn't exactly sure he'd do it, but I always hoped he would. He were never happy here. Started to leave the day he was born."

"You know, he always kept a picture of the road out of Arkansas taped to the inside of his closet door. In fact," I tell her, "it's still there."

"They'd have destroyed him, had he stayed," she says. "Made him into another Norm. It was okay for Norm. It come natural for him to be dull. It would have taken a lot of damage to make Zero as boring as his brother. I guess now he's not around to fight back, Edie can set to work changing his life story to match her country club fantasy." She shakes her head thoughtfully. "Yer right, that woman never be happy until she got everybody twisted her way. Then she still not be happy.

"She give that sweet Zero boy no rest. At him all the time trying to make him like his brother. Slappin' him, pullin' at his hair, screamin'.

"And I tell you, it was his daddy, that crazy man, and he is a very crazy man, that was his salvation." She chuckles, wisely. "Charles MacNoo, nutcase. Crazy? You bet, crazy as a fox!

"He weren't really mad then, not so you could tell much, but he

Varmints!

was always sweet-natured and stood up for Zero in the face of that harpy. And it was him that introduced Zero to that there show biness that he loved, takin' him to the shows down at the Robinson Auditorium and lettin' him go to New York City with his brother, that old fancy boy, Marcus.

"I gotta hand sumthin' to old Edie, though. Zero musta inherited her spunk or he'd never have been able to hold his own. And he always said, she did teach him to write well.

"Yeah, there are days I almost feel sorry for her. There be sumthin' almost heartbreakin' about such a desperate, empty soul. Yes, I almost feel sorry, but then I remembers what a nasty piece of work she can be and I figures she probably deserves all the guilt and grief she's probably feeling now."

"Nobody deserves the grief, Stellrita," I say.

She thinks about that a moment. "You may be right," she replies softly. "Maybe I just gone too hard-hearted. One hundred and twenty-odd years can harden you up considerable regardin' the human condition. Y'all may be lucky to be runnin' out of time in this world, David. Another eighty years and you might end up as crazy and mean as me. Stuck on a porch somewhere, swattin' flies, drinkin' hooch, terrorizin' all and sundry, and tryin' to live with too many memories."

"Well, I'd sure like to have the option," I respond. The day has caught up with me. I can hardly keep my eyes open.

"Y'all go on out to the back and tuck yerself in," she orders. "I'se gonna sit out here a time and have me a conversation with Zero."

"Lance's bus is very late," I observe.

"Don't you worry," she tells me. "I'll send him back directly he arrives. You try to get some rest. I suspect y'all are gonna need it." She leers wickedly and gives me wink. She reaches up and gives my hand a little squeeze. "Go on now, child," she says.

* * *

137

LABOUR OF LOVE

The back shed is comfortable. There's a soft light and a big bed with a patchwork comforter turned down. I throw myself across the bed. I think I'll just close my eyes for a minute. I'm gone in an instant. Through a haze of dreams I hear his soft knock. He's already in the room by the time my eyes are open.

He looks at me in shock. I've lost twenty precious pounds since we saw each other last. I try to joke about it.

"I told you I was disappearing . . ."

"Sssssh," he says, finger to his lips, as he walks across the room to me. He stands before me. Reaches out and traces my brow with his finger, runs it along my cheekbone. His finger is like fire. He cups my face in his warm hands. I kiss his wrist.

"Baby, I'm so glad you're here," I gasp. I can barely breathe.

"I'm so glad you're still here. I was afraid, somehow, you'd be gone," he whispers. His mouth finds mine and all the wild fire banked inside ignites.

We wrestle to the floor. Shirt buttons pop; zippers jam. We pause. For a moment. Breathless.

"Do you have a condom?" he pants.

"Always," I reply.

"I want you inside me, David. Right now."

And, oh, how I want to be there! I fumble in the pocket of my jeans and retrieve a rubber. I curse softly when my pocket spills change across the floor as I dig for the little packet of lube I know is there as well. Aahh! There it is.

I sit up. Kneel between his legs as I roll the condom down to the base of my cock.

"Hurry, baby," he croons. He draws his knees back to his chest. He's smiling. I lube the condom, then take the rest of the grease and spread it on the soft ring of his anus. My finger traces softly round. Slips briefly in. He groans. Slides his legs up on my shoulders. I push into the pulsing heat of his ass. He closes around me. Moaning.

"I think we're ready," he gasps. He slips his hands down my

back. Grabs my butt and pulls me into him. Hard. I slide all the way in. I stop. I try not to move, wanting to feel the fullness of our connection. We kiss. Big. Wet. I feel his fat cock against my belly. We start to rock together.

"Okay, baby, let's go to town!" he growls.

We get where we're going in a hurry. I hold his cock tightly in my hand as it erupts across him. His ass convulses on my dick. I pull out of him.

"No! No, baby, stay!" he pleads. I tear off the rubber and shoot. My cum mingles with his, on his belly and his chest. We are shouting and laughing. I collapse on top of him.

And then the tears come. Great, hot, searing tears that seem like they'll never end. He holds me tight. Kisses the wetness from my face. His lips and tongue soft against the hot flow. It's all the aching trapped in my heart by Zero's going. All my joy in Lance. I'm lost and found. I press against him and weep. Finally, I'm reduced to dry, racking sobs. Then silence.

He rolls away from me. Gathers me in his arms and carries me to the bed. "Lie still, baby," he says.

I watch him through the open door as he cleans the cooled and drying cum at the sink. He returns with a hot washcloth and a towel. Gently, as though he's tending a wound, he cleans me too.

He stretches out behind me and cradles me in his arms. We both sleep briefly. I wake with him curled, spoonlike, against my back. I feel the warm throb of his cock, as it lengthens between my thighs. I push back against him. I feel his lips on my neck. He laughs deep in his throat.

"Do you have another condom?" he murmurs. "I think it's my turn."

I wake to a mockingbird singing outside in the pecan tree. Sunlight spills through the scarlet honeysuckle vine at the window. Lance's head is nestled against my chest. His eyes are already open. He's watching me. He smiles real big. Says, "Sweet man, this is where I've been wanting to be. I have been aching for you. Every which way. If I were to follow you home, would you keep me?"

"You know I would!" I squeeze him tightly. Suddenly I feel serious. "I still haven't figured out how to make that happen. I don't know if I could live with the constant threat of you being deported."

"I wish we could just get married," he says.

"Yeah, that would certainly solve the sponsorship problems," I reply.

He looks so pensive and sad. God, how I've missed this man. I pull him closer to me. "Would it really be fair to you?" I ask. "You're young, you're healthy, you've got the world by the tail. I have no idea how long I've got. I've just lost Zero. I don't think I'm much of a deal for anyone these days. I feel kind of lost in all this stress and fatigue and grief."

He flares up. "Don't be such a jerk, David, and stop feeling so sorry for yourself. I'm not playing a game here. I love you and I want to be with you. I'm an adult. I can make those kinds of decisions."

I weigh this. He burrows his head against me. I feel tears on my chest. I take a deep breath. "Yeah, I want to be with you too. But understand I may need awhile. I'm pretty battered. I may need some solitude to find out the shape of my life without Zero in it."

"I know that, David. It's cool. I need to finish school, and we still haven't figured out how you're going to get me into Canada. Where is Harriet Tubman now that I need her?"

"It would all be so simple if we could find someone to marry you," I lament.

Suddenly for both of us the penny drops. "Frenchie!" we exclaim in unison.

"Do you really think she would?" he asks. He's excited.

"She's almost always game for anything. I don't know why I never thought of this before. Let's ask her."

Varmints!

An hour later, we broach the subject as we sit around the table in the big kitchen.

"Crackerjack idea!" Frenchie exclaims. "I'd be proud to be your spouse, Mister Howard. I thought you'd never ask. Now, when and where shall the deed be done?"

"Do it here," Helen suggests. "Then Lance can probably make application through the Canadian consulate in New Orleans."

"Is there one, Mom?" asks Lance.

"There must be. If not there, probably Houston. There's gotta be one."

Things are moving quickly. "But who's going to marry them on such short notice?" I ask Helen.

"I've no idea. It might be tricky," she replies. "So many of the church folk around here are such tight-assed Bible-thumpers."

"How about a justice of the peace?" asks Frenchie.

"Yeah, that'd probably work," Helen muses. Suddenly, she brightens. "There is that weird Puckett girl, Loopee. She and her sister Jeepers are old school chums of Zero's. They were the two gals in the big blue hats at the cemetery. Loopee is some kind of minister. They just live over on Izzard."

"I know them," Lance says. "They're weird, but real sweet."

"Yeah, a lot like their daddy," says Helen wistfully. "Beebo Puckett. He was a famous local magician. He really was well known. He did 'The Red Skelton Show' or something a long time ago, and he was the toast of Little Rock. He's been dead awhile, though.

"Why don't I give Loopee a call and see if she'd be willing and able to wed 'em on short notice?" She heads for the next room.

We're all giddy with the possibilities of the moment. Helen returns, smiling.

"Well, I explained things to Loopee and she's very happy to be of service. She says to give 'em an hour or so to clean the place up, then to go on over."

LABOUR OF LOVE

Lance whoops. Frenchie leaps to her feet to do a little chicken dance. I just smile. I'm too tired to do much else.

An hour and a half later we pull up in front of a small blue clapboard house on Izzard. There is a big sign on the lawn proclaiming, "Church of The Holy Magic. Weddings, Funerals, Bar Mitzvahs. Tent and Auditorium Shows. Sunday School. Children's Parties. No job too odd or too small! In Jesus Name. The Right Reverend L. Puckett, Handmaiden of the Lord." There's something vaguely familiar about this. Then I remember my ride on The Happy Little Sunday School Bus. And, indeed, there it is, grinning wickedly from the garage beside the porch. The luscious Auto is nowhere to be seen.

The Puckett sisters are sitting on a swing on the front porch, lazily fanning themselves with their big blue hats. Stellrita, who has insisted on coming along, hobbles up the walk at the head of our little party. She peers up at them from the foot of the steps.

"I have no idea which of y'all is which. I never really seen y'all up close since y'all was sprouts. Was right fond of yer daddy, though. Real handsome man, but a bad magician as I recall. My Helen was right sweet on him there for a while. So who's who?"

Lance elbows his mother. Helen giggles softly.

The sisters stand. The taller one extends her hand. "How do, Miz Stellrita? My name is Louette, the Right Reverend Louette Puckett, but you know everybody calls me Loopee. And this here is my sister and sidekick, Jewelle. We call her Jeepers."

The rest of us introduce ourselves.

"So who's gettin' married?" Loopee inquires.

Frenchie and Lance step forward hand in hand. "What a lovely bride!" says the Right Reverend.

"Why, thank you," simpers Lance, striking a pose. Stellrita glares at him.

"Well, let's get on inside and do it," Loopee suggests. We file

Varmints!

into the steaming interior of the bungalow. She leads us into a small room off the hall. On the door is a hand-lettered sign designating it as "The Chapel of Love and Sweet Repose."

The walls are covered with old posters and yellowing news clippings of a very handsome man who I presume is Beebo Puckett. He is invariably shown pulling foreign objects out of the ears and noses of startled children or Rotarians. Headlines indicate that he was a smash sensation the length and breadth of the great state of Arkansas. The toast of the Razorbackers from Judsonia to Buffalo City, Bauxite to Arkadelphia, Toadsuck to Hickeytown.

"Our daddy!" Reverend Loopee indicates with a grand flourish of her hand.

The Right Reverend Loopee flips open a little, hard-bound book on her lectern. It isn't a Bible. The title embossed on the cover announces instead that it is *Meditations on the big Questions*, by The Right Reverend Louette Puckett, Handmaiden to the Lord. She indicates that Frenchie and Lance should stand in front of her. She proceeds to read them a very short piece that seems to borrow heavily from the wisdom of Kahlil Gibran. Then I swear she says, "Abracadabra, shazzam!" and pronounces them husband and wife.

"Now let's get the paperwork done so you can be on yer way. Dern! Where's that nuisance, Jeepers?" She sticks her head out in the hall and shouts, "Jeepers! Where the sam heck are you? Yer supposed to be in here witnessin', girl."

"Comin', Loopee," Jeepers sings out. She bustles in from the back with a big tray of sandwiches, slices of lemon cake, and a frosty pitcher of ice tea. "Just thought these folks might want to set a moment."

"Why, that's mighty sweet of you, Miz Jeepers," says Helen.

The papers are signed in short order. The next hour flies, as we laugh and visit on the stoop.

It's time for us to go. Lance asks what the cost will be. He fumbles for his wallet.

143

"Oh, never mind. This one's on the house!" Loopee declares expansively. "It was my pleasure. Y'all just give me a kiss, and we'll call it square." Lance protests. But she insists.

When we rise to leave she gives Lance a quick peck, but plants what appears to be a much longer and wetter kiss directly on Frenchie's mouth. Frenchie looks startled.

The sisters wave vigorously as we climb into the van. Frenchie still looks flustered.

"What happened, Frenchie?" I ask.

"I'll be damned if the Right Reverend didn't slip me some tongue!" she replies.

Back at Stellrita's, Helen disappears into the cool recesses of the house. Frenchie stretches out on the porch swing. Stellrita hunkers down in her rocker. Within seconds, both of them are snoring loudly.

Lance takes my hand and leads me to the back. "I gotta leave this evening," he says with a woebegone look. "I've got an exam tomorrow afternoon and I want to be sure I ace it. I don't want anything getting in the way now of me comin' north."

"You're pretty optimistic now, aren't you?" I say.

"I feel it in my bones. I know this is going to work."

"Well, it did work eventually for getting Zero into Canada. I don't know why I didn't think of it before. Mental block, I guess."

"I need to have a good talk with Kenny, too," he says.

Kenny's the friend he's been spending time with on campus at Tulane. I never expected Lance to be a nun while we were apart. But I've seen a Polaroid of the lovely Kenny and must confess to a fleeting pang of jealousy at the mention of his name.

He gives me a reassuring squeeze. "Kenny always knew that as soon as you and I could work this out, he and I were over. We'll stay friends. We've had lots of fun together."

"Still, it can't be that easy for him."

"I know," Lance replies, "I have to remember that. I've got you to look forward to." He gets pensive, then brightens. "But he's a real sweet guy, and cute as a bug, too. He'll do okay."

I try to make a joke. I guess it's not a very good one. "Well, don't burn all your bridges, Lance. The way I've been struggling lately, I might not last through this immigration process."

He's not amused. "Shut up, David. You know, for someone who has such a reputation for being smart, you sure can be stupid. Of course, this is all a risk, but I thought we agreed we were going to risk it. But you're right, we don't have time to waste."

"I don't, anyway," I reply.

"Neither one of us does," he says firmly.

He unbuttons my shirt and skins it off me. His big wet tongue licks across my chest to my nipple. I moan deep in my throat, and run my hands over his shoulders and down the silkiness of his back. He moves his lips up to mine. I clasp the full weight and heat of him against the length of me, the sweet hot coffee of his skin scalding mine.

Helen calls softly at the door. "Son, you have a bus to catch in two hours. You boys get yourselves freshened up and come on in and eat some supper. Don't let him dawdle, David."

"No problem," I respond. But it is a problem. I can't keep my hands off him, nor he me. We giggle and play, neither wanting this to end. Not wanting to be apart. Both knowing that for now that's how it has to be. Finally, though, we sober up and struggle into our clothes.

"You still sure you want to risk this, baby?" I ask as we head for the big house.

"Couldn't be surer," he declares, squeezing my hand.

* * *

145

LABOUR OF LOVE

Helen has laid out a feast. Cold fried chicken, collard greens, pepper ham from Mount Petit Jean, mashed potatoes, gravy, black-eyed peas. A huge peach pie sits on the sideboard. Helen, Frenchie, and Stellrita are already at the table.

"Thought I was going to have to go back there and throw a pail of cold water on you two," Stellrita growls. "It's too damned hot for that devilish play. Besides, I'm starvin'. So hungry, I think I can almost choke down some of yer mother's cookin', Lance."

Helen shakes her head and rolls her eyes.

"Grandma, you stay off my mamma's back. You're darn lucky she's here. She takes real good care of you," Lance protests.

"Don't need no lectures from you, boy," snaps Stellrita. She waves him to the seat beside her.

We tuck into the food with a will. Helen keeps a wary eye on the clock. After the last huge pieces of pie have been consumed, she pours us each a glass of elderberry wine and proposes a toast.

"To new beginnings and good endings. To all our fine friends, lost and found. I hope we're all together again soon."

"Mighty soon, or I likely won't be here," mutters Stellrita.

The glasses are raised, clinked, and drained.

"Amen!" says Stellrita.

"Abracadabra, shazzam!" adds Frenchie.

"Heavens!" exclaims Helen, catching sight of the clock again. "Lance, you have fifteen minutes to make that bus. I don't know if you're going to make it!"

"No problema. I'm drivin'," declares Frenchie. "He'll make it."

We pile into the van. Stellrita declines to come. "Don't like good-byes," she announces, settling herself in her rocker. "Besides, all this gallivanting around has just about wore me out."

" 'Bye, Grandma!" Lance calls out as we speed away. She shakes her fist at him.

The bus is about to pull out as we drive up. Frenchie screeches to a halt in front of it to buy us a minute. There are hurried farewells all around. I carry Lance's bag to the bus.

"Hurry up, boy," the driver admonishes.

Lance hands him his ticket, then turns back to plant a lingering kiss on my mouth. His fellow travelers look on in pop-eyed horror and amusement.

"This should be a real fun ride," he says. Then he's up on the top step. He flashes me a wicked smile and disappears inside. The door slams behind him. I see him toss his bag on the overhead rack. He settles beside a grizzled woman who eyes him with a frozen look of terror. He whispers something in her ear and gives her a devilish smile. She doubles over with laughter. He blows me a kiss and he's gone.

"We better hit the road tonight ourselves," says Frenchie, as we head back to the house.

"Tonight?"

"Yeah, I called earlier, and Vargas is getting edgy about how long I've been gone."

"Can't you stay over and get an early start in the morning?" asks Helen. "I think you both need some rest. David still looks real tired."

"Well, we could," French replies, "but I love night drivin', and I'm all jazzed up to go, so if David's up to it, I would like to hit the road."

"It's been such a great time, having y'all here," says Helen wistfully. "I want to thank you for helping Lance with this wedding thing, Frenchie. I sure do hope it works." She wraps her arms around me and gives me a hug. "You make my son real happy, David. That pleases me a whole lot.

"And, you know, except for her rabies scare earlier this year, it's the first time Mother's been off her porch for any length of time since the MacNoo Family Capital Hotel Shoot-Out. She's been havin' a grand old time since you showed up. She's been up and down like a cricket on a hot griddle these past few days. It's good for her." She smiles. "Gives me a bit of a break, too."

She musses my hair. "Sure wish y'all could stay a little longer."

"Thanks, Helen, but Frenchie is probably right, and she is the driver."

"I know, it's just wishful thinking on my part," she sighs.

Back at the house, Frenchie has already got her bag packed. She heaves it in the van.

"Are we leaving this very moment?" I exclaim.

"No, don't panic," she assures me. "While you were sleepin', the Right Reverend Loopee called over here. She said she felt that I might be in need of some spiritual guidance. I told her no, but that I would meet her for a drink. I suggested Discovery II. That didn't seem to faze her, so I'm going to motor over to Discovery directly and seek some spiritual solace with the Handmaiden of the Lord. Be back to fetch you 'round midnight. Get some rest!" She pokes her head out of the window and shouts "Abracadabra, shazzam!" as she drives away.

Helen, Stellrita, and I sit in silence on the porch. Finally, Helen gets up, plants a kiss on my forehead, and says, "I've got to work tomorrow, David, and I'm totally bushed."

"Well, thank you for everything."

"Sure hope we get to see you here again soon," she replies.

"Don't know about that, Helen."

"Yeah, why would he bother?" snarls Stellrita. "He's carryin' off the last of our menfolk. He's got no call to come back here now," she mutters.

"Maybe you could come up to visit us in Toronto, Helen. You'd always be welcome," I offer.

"Maybe," she replies. "I think I'd like that. Goodnight, all."

"Won't find me visitin' no damn Toronto!" declares Stellrita.

Varmints!

"Too far. I may never leave this porch again. Just sit here till I rot and the wind blows my miserable remains to the far corners of this stupid state!"

"Sure hope that's not too soon," I say.

"Can't be soon enough for me!" she snaps. "I look back at my life and what do I see? Years and years of time, all mixed up and crazy. I kinda remembers people, and chances are if they from 'round here, I birthed 'em, and probably nursed 'em with my own titties. I see 'em like they was in a moving picture show, the moment they was born; when they first went to school; first soiled their bedsheets with sex; first married; first child; and it just keeps speedin' up. Then, it starts all over again. I've seen too much. I've had my day.

"There'll be just me 'n' Helen left here soon. I know I'm harder on her than I should be. Always have been. She just ain't a comfort to me. She tries, but it just won't work. Happens sometimes, can't nobody help it.

"But she is here. And she does let me do it my own way. I gotta hand it to her. I'm no picnic to put up with.

"Lord, child, it's just that most everybody in my mind is gone. Most peoples I know are already on the other side. They callin' to me. They say 'Stellrita, what are you waiting for?' I wish I knew, child. Lord, I wish I knew. I've put in my time. I put in my time *double.*"

She squishes her feet in her ever-present bucket of mud. "I may not be here much longer, but I'll stay in touch. You just pay attention." Suddenly she goes very quiet. "Can you hear that?"

"No." I'm perplexed. "Is it the river?"

"No, not that sorry thing. It's in this here mud. Listen close. It's the shuffle slap of pink-soled feet on the banks of the Arkansas. It sounds to me like they be dancin'."

"Now," she continues, "I know y'all got the real Zero in that green velvet bag." The old weasel's been going through my pack! "I also know that I instructed y'all not to bring him back here, but y'all did anyway and I forgives you. But in the future y'all would be wise to pay attention when I come talkin' to you in yer dreams. I'll have you know, it ain't easy making those connections."

"Yes, ma'am."

"Since y'all done brung him all this way, do me a favor. Sift a bit of that sweet Zero on me."

"In your mud?" I ask.

"No. Are y'all deaf or sumthin'? On me, I said."

I dig the bag of ashes from out of my pack. I loosen the drawstring. I plunge my hand in and remove a handful of ashes.

The van roars up to the curb. Frenchie calls out in a loud whisper, "Are you ready to roll?"

"Yeah, give me a minute."

"Sure thing, sport!"

I sprinkle Stellrita gently with the ashes. Her smile is blissful.

"Oh, yes, yes, yes. More! That surely be my Zero. Now y'all get outa here. I need to be alone with him now. Y'all took up too much of my precious time already. Keep that Frenchie outa trouble. And thanks for lookin' after my boy. My boys. Y'all took good care of my Zero and loved him for a good long time. I owe you for that. And now you gone and hexed my Lance as well.

"I 'spect I be dead my ownself soon, so don't fret about me. I done my time. Now get! Take that Zero boy out of this hellhole. Leave me here with the sweet memories of my boy and get the rest of him where he needs to go. You and yer buddies took such good care of him this far, so see it through. Take him to all those places that he loved and where he was loved.

"And David, y'all look worn out yer ownself. You need to get this stuff over and done with and start to look after yerself. You gotta keep yerself alive and well, boy, 'specially if Lance is gonna get him his Canada papers.

"And remember, always want more, child. That's how we survive. Desire. And the ability to forget pain. Now get outa here."

Varmints!

"Yes, ma'am." I blow her a kiss. She glowers at me. I grab my bag and trot across the yard to the van.

I look back as we roar off down the street. For a moment, I can't see her on the darkened porch. Then the moonlight catches her. The ashes gleam, faintly phosphorescent. I can see her lips moving—a silver gnome deep in conversation with the night.

"How'd it go with Loopee?" I ask.

"It went fine," Frenchie replies. "She is a dyke and an active one, too. Being a lesbian or gay activist in Little Rock cannot be an easy row to hoe. I admire her. She's spunky, kind of weird, but funny, too. She's threatening to load up some of the sisters here and bring them up to Toronto, for what she says would be a spiritual excursion."

"Did you get any more of that tongue?" I query.

"You betcha!" she hoots. "Abracadabra, shazzam!"

I quickly nod off to sleep. I swim back to consciousness a couple of hours later. We're pulled over to the side of the road beneath a solitary streetlight at a junction.

"What are we doing?" I ask.

"Where was it you wanted to take the rest of those ashes?" she inquires casually.

"San Francisco, Saskatchewan," I reply groggily.

"Well, let's go then. Let's take Zero where he needs to go. Like the old woman said."

"Frenchie, you're already in deep shit about this van!" I protest, beginning to really wake up.

"My point precisely!" she declares. "Might as well go the whole nine yards. And hell, we're already halfway there."

"But, Frenchie . . ."

151

LABOUR OF LOVE

"Listen, sport, you're too exhausted and stressed out right now to be arguing with the likes of me, so don't even start. Just relax and see America. I feel like drivin'!"

The G-force of her takeoff pins me back hard against my seat. We're headed West.

THE LONG WAY HOME

She's right. I am exhausted. Profoundly, deeply exhausted. Bone-weary. The Midwest flies by at high speed. There are fleeting stops for greasy food and hot corrosive coffee in anonymous diners. I'm in suspended animation, slipping in and out of dreams. She rarely sleeps. Occasionally she pulls over to the shoulder of the road and curls up with me on the air mattress in the back.

It's a glorious morning when we pull into Sausalito. The fog is just lifting and The City sparkles. Oz. San Francisco, for years my second home. The place where Zero and I shared so many fine times. We'd even lived here awhile in our early years.

We cross the Golden Gate Bridge. I get Frenchie to stop at the first phone booth.

I call my dear old friend, Tom Quinlan. He's surprised to hear from me. Even more surprised that I'm so near. He and Zero were close. Real close.

"Listen, Tom," I say, "I really need a chance to rest up and catch my breath. I want to leave some of Zero's ashes on the beach beneath the bridge, but I don't think I can tackle that hill without some real sleep. And I think the mad woman, Frenchie, who's chauffeuring me, must be absolutely dead on her feet. Can you put us up for a day or so?"

LABOUR OF LOVE

"Of course!" Tom is very excited. "You can stay with us for-ever, if you have to. You know you're always welcome."

We arrange to meet at the Cafe Flore, in an hour. This is all new to Frenchie. She's quickly wired, what with the strong cappuccino and the excitement of the motley traffic at the cafe. Tom bounds up. I introduce him to Frenchie.

"Listen," he says, "I'm double-parked. Do you want to stay here or should we just head on over to our place right now, so you can really relax?"

"Do you have a bathtub?" asks Frenchie.

"Sure do, long and deep."

"Then we're going to your place. I need a long, hot soak. I must smell like a goat."

"Me, too," I say.

"Okay, let's go."

Tom lives in the Upper Haight area, on Downey Street. Zero and I had lived in the same house during our time in The City. The neighborhood is crowded with familiar landmarks, with memories. As usual, parking is a nightmare, but we manage.

Tom and his boyfriend, Boojum, share the second floor of the old building with an old gray collie called Willy, and a truly giant Samoan named Louise. She must be seven feet tall. They immediately make us welcome.

I lie down on the couch. Louise runs Frenchie a bath, then bustles off to the kitchen. She returns after a few minutes with a list of groceries for Tom and Boojum to pick up.

"But we want to visit!" they protest.

"Shop now. Visit later," she rumbles. "Look at him. He's white as a sheet. Give him a chance to rest a bit." She shooes them out. "Now, you just close your eyes, honey." She settles beside me on the couch, and takes my head in her huge hands. She strokes my temples. As I float into sleep, I am vaguely aware of Frenchie splashing exuberantly about down the hall. She's singing, at the top of her lungs, "I am Woman, hear me roar . . ."

It's late when I wake. The room I'm in is dark. I can hear them talking quietly in the next room. I wander in, rubbing my eyes. They're all curled up on Tom and Boojum's big bed. Frenchie is regaling them with Arkansas tales. Boojum slips out. I hear the tub begin to fill again. He's back in a few moments.

"I've put out fresh towels for you, David. The blue ones."

"Thanks, Booj."

He gives me a little kiss. Boojum and I were boyfriends a long time ago, before I even met Tom or Zero. We've never lost our attraction for each other. We haven't done anything about it for a few years, but it's reassuring to know it's still there.

I slip into the deep old tub, sinking into the drifts of steaming bubbles. I can feel knots unlocking deep in my flesh. I close my eyes. Let my mind go blank.

Boojum comes in after a while and offers to wash my hair.

"They're setting the table. So dinner's on the way," he informs me.

He sits on the edge of the tub, lathering up my hair. He hums quietly as his long fingers knead my scalp. This is heaven.

"Remember when you and I and Zero all crammed into this old tub?" I ask.

He chuckles. "We were wild boys."

"Tom was so pissed off when he came home and found us hard at play."

"He was just mad because he'd missed most of the action," he giggles.

"Yeah, because he was off fucking with his little friend Herbie, from the food co-op on Haight Street."

157

LABOUR OF LOVE

"Wild boys, for sure," he says, wistfully. He shakes his head. "If we only knew then what we know now."

"Hell, Booj, we didn't and we couldn't, and I, for one, have no regrets. Yeah, I'd do it differently now, but I'd still do it. I wouldn't trade all those wonderful times for anything."

"Nor would I, but so many of our friends and playmates are gone now," he says pensively, as he rinses my head.

"Yeah, and I wish we could get them back. But we can't."

He makes me stand up. Rubs me down with a thick towel.

"Still love getting my hands on you, sweet man," he murmurs, lingering with the towel at my groin. He bends down and kisses the rapidly hardening head of my cock. My head reels with the sudden dizzy heat of the moment. I grab his shoulder to steady myself.

Tom calls from the hallway, "Now you two old whores don't get started in there. Boojum, you behave!" We all laugh. Boojum pats my ass and heads for the kitchen.

I slip back into my jeans and pull on a fresh T-shirt. Then I join them.

Louise is wearing a giant, brightly flowered muumuu. The big kitchen table is crowded with food. Candles flicker everywhere. The others are just sitting down when I join them. Tom gives me a wink.

"Would you like a pillow for that skinny little butt of yours?" he asks.

"Actually, I wouldn't mind," I reply. "I'm just sitting on a memory these days."

"But what a great memory!" he hoots.

Over the feast, Frenchie and I fill them in on the events of the past months. The memories I'd put on hold in the headlong rush to Arkansas, and in our whirlwind flight across the heartland, come crowding back. As hard as they are, though, it feels right to share them here, with good old friends, full of fine food, warmed by the glow of candlelight and wine.

"So, what are the plans?" asks Tom.

The Long Way Home

"Well, like I said, I want to take some ashes to that little beach beneath the Golden Gate Bridge," I reply.

"Wow, David, that hill is a long, steep, treacherous climb in the best of times. Are you ready for it?" inquires Boojum, his voice full of concern.

"No, it should just about kill me. I'll need to take my time," I answer.

"And then we'll probably hit the road again," declares Frenchie. "We've still got a lot of miles to cover, and I'm in serious shit over this journey already."

Tom shakes his head. "You guys are absolutely nuts. It completely wears me out, thinking about you two tearing back and forth across the continent."

He turns to Frenchie and says sternly, "He's been through hell. What if he gets sick?"

"He was sick," she replies.

"What did you do?" asks Louise.

Frenchie guffaws. "I left him in a ditch somewhere outside of West Memphis. What else?" By the time she's explained my adventures with the Mud Folk, we are all doubled over laughing. I'm afraid Louise will sustain a physical injury.

After we calm down a bit, Frenchie yawns. Big. "Can someone show me to a bed? These tired old bones need to lie down," she says sleepily.

"Sure thing, Frenchie," says Louise, rising to her feet. "Right this way. I've put a down comforter on the bed. It gets surprisingly cool here at night. And there's a collective delusion in San Francisco that since this is California it must be warm, so most of these houses aren't insulated."

I rise to help Boojum and Tom clear the table and clean the dishes.

"No, David, you stay right where you are," orders Boojum.

"It's so good to see you," says Tom. "But I can't believe that crazy dyke has dragged you all over hell's half acre with those damned ashes. I can't help but be worried about you. You look very, very tired, honey."

"I am. You can't begin to know how tired," I reply wearily. "But this journey has been a godsend. I needed to be away, and this has taken me out of that house. It's also kept me preoccupied, beyond the immediacy of my grief. I've had some great laughs and new adventures. I'm getting to see old friends like you guys, just when I most need to see them. And, quite frankly, this is the pace I've lived at for a long time."

"Yeah, sweetie, but you've got to slow down," says Tom. "We want the pleasure of your company for a good long time yet."

"No guarantee on that," I answer, with a smile. "It is really wonderful, though, to see you both. Oh, by the way, did you receive an invitation for October thirteenth? Zero always wanted a party, so his friends could celebrate his life. We've scheduled it in a couple of weeks. It's your Columbus Day long weekend, our Canadian Thanksgiving. It would be great if you could come," I say hopefully.

"We did get the invitation," Tom responds.

"God, I'd love to be there, but it's very doubtful that I could get away," Boojum adds.

"Don't tell me, you have all that to organize when you get home!" says Tom, looking cross again.

"No, Searcy and Snookums are in complete control of the situation." I touch wood. "At least, they were when we left."

The dishes are glistening in the rack. The candles are guttering out, one by one. Boojum and Tom share a joint. The conversation is lazy. Desultory.

"Well, tomorrow's going to be a long one," I say, rising. "Will one of you kind gentlemen show me to my chambers?"

Boojum puts out the remaining candles, with the exception of a large white votive.

The Long Way Home

Tom puts his arm around me and says, "You're coming with us."

In their room, the three of us undress each other in the candle's glow. There's no haste, no urgency to this, just occasional giggles, soft moans, and the wet smack of lazy kisses. We slip beneath the duvet. Twine together and roll about like puppies in a languid sexy jumble. Playful. Warm. Half-asleep. I'm sandwiched between the boys. The wine, the weight of the world, and the gentle push and pull of these familiar, friendly bodies take me to my dreams.

Tom slips out at dawn to cycle to the marina for his morning swim. Boojum and I snuggle more tightly together to fill the gap he's left behind.

"This sure feels good," Boojum whispers. "But then it always has."

"Almost too good. You'd better be careful. I'll be moving in here before you know it."

"I'd like that. You know we'd love that to happen. Seriously."

"Thanks, Booj."

We play for a while, still only half-awake. I love re-exploring the delicious terrain of his lanky beauty.

"Jeez!" he exclaims, catching sight of the clock. "I better get breakfast going. Tom will be back soon and he'll be ravenous. I've got to be at work in an hour, and you have a very tough day ahead of you. Real life," he complains, "always getting in the way." He squirms lazily against me, reluctant to disengage. And so am I.

"We better not start again," I pout, rolling him off me.

"You're right. It feels so good, though."

"Sure does." I swat the luscious muscle of his butt as he bends over by the bed searching for his jeans.

"You stay cozy for a few more minutes there," he commands. "I need to take a shower. Then I'm afraid it's pancakes for you, pal."

LABOUR OF LOVE

"Wonderful!" I exclaim. Boojum made me pancakes the first morning we met, more than fifteen years ago. It's been our tradition through the years.

I wait till he's finished in the bathroom, then slip in for a quick shower. The needle points of the scalding water leave me invigorated, alive, ready to tackle the day's task. I dress quickly, shivering in the chill morning air, then head down the hall to the kitchen.

Boojum is vigorously mixing his batter. He stops to hand me a mug of coffee. He plants a whiskery kiss on my lips. "Frenchie and Louise are in the garden," he reports. "We'll eat out there."

I kiss the back of his neck as he turns back to his bowl.

The garden is lush. "It's great, isn't it?" says Louise. "The boys are both such good gardeners. It's something I do not have a gift for. How was your night?" she asks with a sly smile.

I grin back. "Lovely. And how was yours?"

"Exhausting."

"Exhausting?"

"Yes, I've been working the midnight shift at San Francisco General this week. I've actually just gotten home. I'm dead on my big feet."

"What do you do?" asks Frenchie.

"I nurse. In the AIDS ward," Louise responds, with a weary, gentle smile. "I love what I'm doing, but it's a killer."

"I bet," I say.

"How did you end up living with Tom and Boojum?"

"Oh, I met Boojum a long time ago, when he was just a kid," she replies. "I was working the emergency room in Butte, Montana, one night when this unbelievably handsome kid staggered in, clutching his shoulder. He was bleeding like a stuck pig. Someone had shot him!

"I dressed the wounds and asked him what had happened. He was fifteen years old. He said he'd known he was gay for four or five years. Thought it was time to share the news with his mom. He actually thought she'd be okay. She wasn't.

"She heard him out, then fished her handgun out of her purse and tried to gun him down. He got out of the house, but she winged him a couple of times as he fled down the driveway. As far as I know, the last time he ever saw his mother she was screaming that he was an abomination and blazing away at him with her six-gun from the front steps. He just ran off into the night, and he's been on his own ever since. He's a great kid."

"He sure is!"

"Well, I patched him up, he left, and I didn't see him again for about ten years. Then I was working here in the VD clinic. He came in for a shot, and we recognized each other immediately. After that, we'd see each other on the street from time to time. We seemed to like each other, and we always spoke.

"Then last winter, when Tom discovered the first KS lesion on his chest, I ran into Booj crying into his beer at The Mint one night. He was pretty drunk, so I helped him home. Met Tom. They were both in kind of rough shape then. Tom, trying to cope with his new reality, and Boojum, trying to cope with Tom's coping. Not a happy time.

"I ended up being here a lot. Every day, in fact. Then, one day, they asked me if I'd like to move in. I jumped at the chance. It's the best decision I ever made. I really love these guys."

"We love you, too, Louise," Boojum sings out from the doorway. "That's enough of my sordid secrets for now, though." He shovels pancakes onto our plates. "Tom's showering, but you guys start on these while they're hot."

We need no encouragement.

* * *

LABOUR OF LOVE

Too soon, Boojum has to run to work.

"Sure wish we could keep you here," he says, with a catch in his voice.

"I'll be in touch soon," I promise.

"You know, if you ever need me, I'll come."

"I know that, Booj, but you've got a full plate here."

"Some days, it's too full," he says ruefully.

"Believe me, I know, Booj. But it could be empty soon enough."

"I try not to think about that."

"Well, he looks good."

"His blood count is steady in the mid-three hundreds, and he's still only got the two small lesions. One on his chest and one on his gums. He's very up most of the time, too. I'm the one who's preoccupied with it. There are days when I almost wish I had tested positive, too. In some ways, it might be easier."

"None of it's easy, Boojum."

"Shit, David, will you listen to me carry on? Forgive me." He's very contrite. "You shouldn't have to listen to my whining after all you've been through."

"Booj, baby, you can whine to me any old time you like," I assure him. "We need to keep talking about it, just to stay sane. Just to stay alive."

"You're right. I know." He pushes his hair back from his forehead. "I just feel like such an ungrateful wimp, so much of the time. Like I don't deserve to have tested negative. How did that happen? We all did the same things, with most of the same people. So how did the virus miss me?"

"You're just a lucky guy. You always did have horseshoes up your ass," I tell him.

"Horsehoes and everything else!" laughs Tom, hurrying down the hallway, pulling on the ancient teal-blue sweater which, patched, and repatched, but still full of holes, he has worn virtually every day of his life since he was fifteen. "Honey, you are going to be so late and you don't want to screw up this job. Come on, I'll drive you."

Boojum's bottom lip is trembling. "I'm out of here, David." They clatter down the stairs. On the final step Boojum turns with a sad, crooked little smile and throws me a kiss.

"Back in a flash," Tom sings out as he disappears out the door.

There is an uproar down the hall. Frenchie has barged in on Louise in her bath. She backs out, apologizing profusely. She's extremely flustered.

As soon as Tom returns, she takes him aside and asks, "Is Louise a man or a woman?"

"Damned if I know," Tom shrugs. "I've never figured that one out. Could be a little bit of both."

"It didn't look like a little bit to me," exclaims Frenchie. "That girl is hung like a horse!"

We decide to take the van and Tom's car. He has a job across the bay in Marin County later this afternoon, and Frenchie is anxious, as always, to be back on the highway. And so am I. The last twenty-four hours have been heavenly, and I truly would like to linger, but I have much to do in far-off places. I need to know that I'm headed home.

Louise wanders out of the bathroom, swathed in a huge bath sheet. She hugs us both good-bye.

"Rest easy," she whispers to me. "I'm taking good care of them."

"Louise is not a man or a woman," I say to Frenchie, as we climb into the van.

"I know," replies Frenchie. "She's an angel."

* * *

LABOUR OF LOVE

They both want to make the trip down the hill with me at Baker Beach. I am resolute.

"I need to do this myself," I insist. "Wait for me here. Visit. Get to know each other better. Admire nature."

"What if you fall down the hill, or run out of steam at the bottom?" asks Tom.

"Listen, if I'm not back in an hour, you can come looking for me," I concede.

They look at each other.

"It's a deal," says Frenchie.

I head down the hill. It's one of those perfect, San Franciscan autumn days. The City's real summer. The sky is pristine. Cloudless. The Golden Gate Bridge arcs its magnificent span across the glittering bay. Nasturtiums spill, wild, on either side of the steep path.

I negotiate the trail down with caution. Finally, I reach the bottom. When I look back, my heart sinks. How will I ever drag these weary bones back up there? Frenchie and Tom are peering anxiously down at me from the top. They see me turn. Reassured, they wave gaily at me and disappear from view.

I sit a moment. Winded. There is the usual handful of naked men basking among the rocks. It's very quiet. The steady pulse of the tide is broken only by the occasional plaintive cries of gulls kiting in the light breeze.

I head off along the beach. This place, too, resonates with memory.

I climb atop a huge outcropping of stone about halfway down. I untie the little bag I've brought down with me and sprinkle Zero's ashes. A light breeze catches them as they fall, scattering them among the rocks and into the frothing edge of the bay.

I climb down and search at the base of the boulder I've been standing on. From among the rocks there, I choose a chunk of serpentine. The stone, dark green, dense with time, fits perfectly in my hand. I drop it into my pack.

The Long Way Home

The last time I was here was a day just like today, bright, hot, sparkling. Zero, Boojum, our wild lesbian friends from Portland, Mudhen and Charlie, and I had made our way down in the late morning, hauling lots of good food and drink. We all shed our clothes as soon as we reached the base of the path.

It was a glorious day. We were all so crazy and beautiful and alive and in love with one another. It was the day I took the picture of Zero flying through the air.

I stand a moment and look out at the water, aching with loss, full of rich remembrance.

My mission in this special place accomplished, I start back up the hill. All the walking and climbing has worn me out once more. I have to stop again and again to catch my breath. Sweat drips into my eyes. I'm laboring up the path, when loose gravel and stones come raining down from above me on the trail. Frenchie and Tom are scrambling down to give me a hand.

"It hasn't been an hour yet," I protest halfheartedly.

"We were worried," they chorus.

"So was I," I pant, laughing at their anxious voices and the concern in their faces. They seem so terribly alarmed.

We are nearer the top than I had imagined. Frenchie takes my hand and virtually drags me the last thirty yards. We collapse together on the bench at the top.

My legs have turned to jelly. I gasp for breath. Tom has run ahead to his car and returns with some of his famous tofu pâté sandwiches, and some mineral water. The hike has left me ravenous and this is a feast.

Frenchie goes to check out the van. As always, she's anxious to be in motion.

"Well, old friend," says Tom, "I won't say good-bye to you. It scares me to do that anymore."

LABOUR OF LOVE

"Yeah, I know what you mean. Let's just promise to keep in close touch. We both still have a long way to go."

"I sure hope that's true," he says, tousling my hair.

I take him in my arms. "Thanks for all this, Tommy," I whisper into the soft golden skin at the side of his neck.

On the road again, I look back at The City as we cross the bridge. The fog is rolling in. I wonder, Will I ever see this place again?

We make good time as we head north through the wine country. The air is heady and full with the smell of ripening grapes. The fields are busy with their picking.

Frenchie seems increasingly agitated now. She needs to be home. She misses her "girls," and Tom's concerns about my condition, and the very real threat of being charged with theft of the van, all conspire to make her edgy. She's grappling, as well, with the wild swings of her ever-changing menopausal state. Today she alternates between hot flashes and chills. Somehow she manages to stay relatively cheerful and exuberant.

We're at a truck stop near Winnemucca, Nevada. Frenchie's already wolfing down her second plate of bacon and eggs. She's driven all night and is looking kind of scary. Frowzy-haired. Wild-eyed. She looks like she might have escaped from somewhere.

"Well, sport, how ya holding up?"

"Fine," I lie. "I'm more concerned about you."

"No problema. I haven't had such a great time in years. Reminds me of my days touring with the Fabulous Wineberg Sisters."

For several years back in the late seventies and early eighties, Frenchie, Hoo Hoo, and Lucy had something of a national notoriety with their à cappella singing trio, the Fabulous Wineberg Sisters. They shaved their heads, donned granny gowns and work boots, and wore Groucho Marx glasses and noses everywhere they went.

The Long Way Home

Their wild harmonies were a mix of outrageously funny satirical ditties and quite stirring, tender ballads which spoke to various wonders and worries of modern life. Zero had even written some material for them, but most of it was their own. He'd also coached them in the intricate vocal harmonies that became their trademark.

None of them sang particularly well, but in combination they were very good. And very funny.

They toured back and forth across Canada in Lucy's station wagon. I actually first met them when they showed up to sing at a rally I had organized in opposition to an Anita Bryant visit to Moose Jaw, Saskatchewan. They'd somehow teamed up with Randy. I think he was their driver, business manager, and general dog's body. That was my first contact with him as well.

They were outrageous on- and offstage, and had really developed a dedicated cult-following all over the country. But I guess the good times got to be a grind. Not enough dollars, poor accommodations, too much booze and bad food. Things were beginning to fray at the edges. One night, Hoo Hoo had enough. She sat them down in their hotel room after a gig in Winnipeg and posed the question. What was more important, their relationship, or the Fabulous Wineberg Sisters?

There wasn't much debate. Frenchie, who had always been the center of attention onstage as the lead singer, wanted to continue. She loved showbiz, life on the road. The other two were tired. They wanted to stop. Faced with the possibility of splitting up their more intimate act, the Winebergs had to go. They did a tumultuous farewell gig at the Cameron Public House on Queen Street in Toronto and retired. Called it quits. They were all nostalgic for their crazy days on tour, none more so than Frenchie.

"Have you got the map?" she asks, as she mops up the last of her eggs with her toast. She jams it into her mouth.

"Yeah, right here in my pack."

LABOUR OF LOVE

"Well, spread it out," she demands. "We need to chart a course." She pores over the well-worn map, absentmindedly eating the toast I've inadvertently put down within her reach.

"Hey, does Dilly still live in Edmonton?" she asks. Dilly is my mother. She and Frenchie met years ago, when the Fabulous Wineberg Sisters gave a concert in my hometown.

"No. She lives north of here, in British Columbia. It's in the Kootenay Valley, just over the border from Idaho. She moved out there this spring. I haven't seen the place yet."

"How did she end up in interior B.C.?"

"Well, you know she'd married my dad, Baldy, when she was really only a kid. Eighteen or nineteen years old. They were together thirty-five years. Never apart. Then, just when he was due to retire, Baldy died. Horribly. With cancer. Mom nursed him through that.

"All of a sudden she was alone, on her own for the first time really. She'd been convent-educated, and had gone directly from that to him. All of us kids were scattered around the country. We had our own busy lives.

"She was immobilized, and although she was still young, only fifty-four, you'd swear that she was closer to eighty. She was rudderless, lonely, and very sorry for herself. To top it off her health began to fail. It was really painful to see her that way.

"She left her comfortable home on the farm and moved to Edmonton. She lived in a cramped apartment within sight of the gigantic West Edmonton Mall. She rarely went out, except to wander the mall. She spent her time watching TV, eating junk food, and drinking too much with other displaced lonely folks in her building. It was sad. She didn't seem to be able to get a handle on her life. She wasn't interested in anything, and she wasn't interesting.

"Then, suddenly last Christmas, my sister called and said, 'Did you know that Mom's been seeing Erv Ramsbottom?'

" 'Erv Ramsbottom? How did that come about? What happened to Florrie?' I asked.

The Long Way Home

"Erv and Florrie had been our neighbors back on the farm. Good friends of our parents. We had grown up with their kids. I'd known them all of my life. They sold their farm twenty years ago and moved out to the West Coast. We kind of lost contact with them after that.

"My sister told me that shortly after they set up their new home, Florrie ran off with a Mormon missionary. Erv was devastated. A lot like Mom. Lost and alone.

"He moved to the Kootenay Valley and lived there by himself for years. Then, according to my sister, his eldest daughter, who had maintained a correspondence with Mom through the years, encouraged her dad to write to Dilly. So he did. Dilly replied. They wrote back and forth. He arranged to visit her in Edmonton. Next thing we knew they were taking little trips together in his recreational vehicle. Then, just at mid-summer, this year, she informed us that she was packing up and moving to B.C. to be with Erv.

"My sister's first reaction was, 'Are you going to become Mrs. Ramsbottom?'

" 'Oh no, Florrie's still his wife. We just plan to live in sin,' Mom giggled.

"I tell you, Frenchie, my mother has been transformed. The two of them are having such a good time together. They both seem to be very happy. You know, at sixty-four, I'm sure she probably thought there'd never be love like this in her life again. I'm just so happy for them both. It's a real gift, that they've found each other."

Frenchie's gone all misty-eyed on me. "What a wonderful story. It's really never too late, is it?"

"No, I guess not."

"Well, if we're so close, why don't we just angle up through Idaho and then kitty-corner across lower B.C., up through Alberta, and across to Saskatoon?" She's planning on the fly. "We could maybe stay overnight. You could check out your mom's new situation, and I'm sure she'd give her eyeteeth to see you."

"Jeez, Frenchie. I don't know. Can you sustain this pace?"

LABOUR OF LOVE

"I can, if you can. Besides, we have to go up that way anyway. It would be a real pity not to see them when they're so close by."

Near Couer d'Alene, Idaho, the engine begins to knock. Frenchie tinkers with it, emerging black and greasy, to announce that we can probably get as far as Mom and Erv's place. She needs tools, though, if she's going to fix it further.

"Well, let's see if we can make it then. Erv is a mechanical wizard and apparently has an excellent machine shop. He should have everything you need. Or, if not, he could build it."

I get Frenchie to stop at a phone booth at some little place south of Bonner's Ferry. Mom is very surprised to hear from me; more surprised to hear that I'm nearly on her doorstep. My sister had told her I was in Arkansas. I tell her about our situation.

"Well, I'm sure Erv can help her fix the van. So you get here as soon as you can. If we're not around, don't panic. We won't have gone far."

She gives me explicit directions to their mountain home.

"It sure will be a treat to see you, son. I've been so worried. I always wish there was something I could do. I mean, really do."

The operator warns me that I'm almost out of time, and I'm almost out of change.

"You better brace yourself, Mom. I'm a lot thinner than the last time you saw me."

"Doesn't matter, son. We'll just fatten you up."

"Yeah, overnight." I laugh.

Again we're waved through the border crossing. No hassles. I must travel with this woman more often. The engine sounds more and more like it's about to blow up.

"Damn!" curses Frenchie. "Now, not only am I going to be

172

charged with car theft, but I'll probably have to replace this pitiful piece of junk as well."

"Well, Frenchie, you have driven the shit out of this thing," I observe.

She glares at me. "I was just trying to burn the carbon out of it," she replies defensively.

"And me as well, I guess," I respond. I'm tired and more than a little peevish. She immediately looks so crestfallen, I relent. I reach over and give her biceps a squeeze. "I'm sorry, Frenchie. I don't mean to give you a hard time."

"Yeah, let's not start fightin' now," she says, as she adjusts her moose hat in the rearview mirror. She flashes me a big grin. "Sure hope old Erv has the tools."

The van chugs and farts as it labors up the hill to my mother's new home. About halfway up, there is a jarring series of loud explosions and the vehicle comes to a shuddering, smoking halt. Frenchie buries her head in her hands. It looks like she's about to burst into tears.

"I can walk the rest of the way up and get some help," I offer.

"No, you can't!" she says testily, pounding the dashboard in frustration.

"Yes, I can," I snap, more than a little testy myself.

A bright red half-ton careens around the corner behind us. Frenchie leaps out of the van, flapping her arms in an effort to catch the driver's eye. The truck speeds on by. Suddenly, it screeches to a stop and reverses at high speed toward us.

"David, it's your mom!" Frenchie yelps.

And so it is.

Mom and Erv climb out of the truck and crunch through the gravel toward us, both grinning like Cheshire cats.

"What bizarre outfits," Frenchie says under her breath, as she adjusts her moose hat to a more rakish angle.

They're wearing matching outfits. Mom's in a mauve dress,

spotted with yellow daisies. She's wearing yards of crinoline. Erv, looking unchanged since I last saw him twenty years ago, sports an Apache tie of the same daisy-bedecked material. The theme is repeated on the band of his enormous cowboy hat. They're holding hands.

Dilly greets us. "You're lucky," she says. "We're just on our way home from our afternoon square dance club." She hugs me hard. Her eyes are full of questions and concern.

"You remember Frenchie, don't you, Mom?" I ask.

"Sure I do," Mom replies, looking rather puzzled. "But weren't you called Olga in those days?"

Frenchie beams, nodding vigorously.

"Anyway, Frenchie, this is my friend, Erv Ramsbottom."

Erv shakes Frenchie's hand, then mine. "Gee willikers, it's good to see you again, son," he exclaims. Then he turns back to Frenchie.

"This here van give out on you?"

"Yeah, I can fix it, though. If I have the tools."

"I've got the tools. Will it run?"

She shakes her head. "Don't think so."

"Let's play it safe then. We'll just throw a logging chain on her and tow her up to the shop."

Dusk has fallen. The autumn air up on the mountain is cold and crisp. Mom and I nurse steaming mugs of peppermint tea at the kitchen table. Frenchie and Erv are out talking machine-talk in the shop. Erv has decided that he has to retool the damaged part. They've been at it for hours now.

"Erv's in heaven," Mom confides. "He loves fixing and building things, and he loves having someone around who's interested and willing to listen to all of his theories. It gives me a bit of a rest, too.

"I thought your father was opinionated, but Baldy couldn't hold a candle to this one in the know-it-all department. He's got an opinion on absolutely everything. Some of it's pretty silly macho stuff, but I just bite my tongue. I know what I know. I've been around awhile. I have my own opinions."

"You do seem happy, Mom."

"Very," she says, "this is where I want to be. And we're having a wonderful time."

"Well, you deserve it," I say, toasting her with my tea.

It's almost midnight when the mechanics stumble in.

"It's done. Purrs like a kitten," announces Erv.

They're both very smug. And very dirty.

"Get cleaned up," Mom commands, "we've been waiting supper on you."

"Oh, honey, you should have gone ahead," Erv protests.

"It's okay. Just hop to it."

She's cooked a huge meal. I can't remember her cooking like this since I was a child back on the farm. I am so happy to see the changes in her life. I feel lifted by her new enthusiasm.

Immediately after we eat, Mom and I retire to the kitchen again. She loads the dishwasher. I'm drifting off. I can barely keep my eyes open. She notices.

"Don't fight it, son. Let me show you to your room. We can visit some more in the morning."

Erv and Frenchie are out in his ham radio shack. He has an extremely sophisticated ham radio and he's busily explaining the complicated arcana of the operation to Ms. La Touche. He is a fascinating and gifted know-it-all, and she's an enthusiastic audience. Quite frankly, all that technical hoo-ha wears me out.

Mom sits on the edge of my bed. "You're headed to Saskatoon tomorrow?"

"First thing, I guess." I explain Frenchie's predicament vis-à-vis the van and her job.

"It would be great if you could stay here with us for a while," she says hopefully.

"I know, Mom, but I just can't."

She shrugs. "I understand, son. It's just wishful thinking. I'm very sorry Erv never had the chance to meet Zero. I think he would have liked him."

"Well, Zero would have enjoyed meeting Erv. He would have thought he was a real interesting character."

She laughs. "And so he is!"

I reach over and take her hand. I tell her, "Zero was real pleased about this new happiness in your life. He was very fond of you."

"Well, I always thought he found me boring. I'm not a very flashy gal. But I was fond of him, too, though it's sometimes hard for me to show it. Even Baldy liked him."

"Well, they both liked to tell tall tales, didn't they?" I say, with a chuckle.

She laughs. "Unkind people would call it lying."

"Do you miss him?" I ask.

"Your dad? Yes, every day in some way, but almost always it's the good stuff. So, most of the time it's okay. Other times, it seems like more than I can bear."

"I know. It's like part of me has been torn away," I tell her. "One of the first things I noticed is how much too big the bed is without Zero there."

"It's funny, because it's not like we hadn't spent time apart over the years. Quite long stretches actually, these past years, with his comings and goings with Clay and Jeff. But I always knew, roughly, where he was. And I always knew, or hoped, he'd be back. And he always was.

"And these last months have been so sweet and fierce, like all the hurt and pain we'd made for each other through the years had been absolved. The lovers' knot we lived in like a second skin had retied itself, even closer and tighter. And we both seemed so hungry for every moment, every point of contact, we could eke out.

"Then, suddenly, he's gone. Really gone. Not just down the street, or upstairs, or on vacation. But gone, forever. And I feel that, like a deep, deep physical pain, as though part of me has been cut away, leaving a hole that only he could ever fill again. And right now, it's the hardest thing to bear."

She nods and sits quietly holding my hand. She rises to leave. "Just remember, son, don't let anyone else tell you how to grieve. We all deal with this differently. And you do it the way you need to, and at your own speed.

"Now, you get some sleep. I want to show you around the acreage before you leave. Sweet dreams."

"Mom," I ask, as she's almost across the room, "would you sing me 'Little Joe, the Wrangler'?"

Throughout my childhood, it seemed my mother was always singing. She had a lovely, clear, sort of forties radio voice. And she was my young and very beautiful mother, and she sang and sang and sang. Ballads, Broadway tunes, cowboy songs, not country and western stuff, but old range and cattle drive songs like "The Old Chisolm Trail," "Old Paint," or "Little Joe, the Wrangler."

This last, about Little Joe fleeing a bad home to acceptance by a rough trail gang and ultimate tragedy in a heroic attempt to stop a herd of stampeding cattle, had always broken our hearts. We'd sit huddled together, tears streaming down our little faces. Absolutely stricken at the brave child's tragic fate.

Even now, at every family gathering we clamor for her to sing it once again. And, always, even as we edge into middle age, it leaves us deliciously sorrowful and weeping. Children once again.

"Gee, son, I don't know, I don't have much voice anymore." She's reluctant but pleased to be asked.

"Please."

LABOUR OF LOVE

She sits back down beside me, takes my hand, and begins to sing, "Little Joe, the wrangler, he'll wrangle never more . . ." Her voice is nearly gone, she's been a relentless and dedicated smoker for forty-five years, but she quavers on through, and the ghost of that beautiful memory is still there. As she nears the graphic rendering of the poor lad's end, "crushed to a pulp," my heart breaks once again. And, so, I guess, it ever shall.

My eyes are already closing when she puts out the light.

It's a gray morning, and cool up here on the mountain. We sit around the kitchen with our coffee. Erv bustles about, busily preparing breakfast. Green apple rings fried up with bacon, crisp waffles, lots of coffee.

He and Frenchie keep up a steady dialogue. She's very excited about the ham radio. I think she wants one. Her next toy.

Mom says, "I forgot, Erv, your hamster friends from Revelstoke are supposed to drop by this afternoon."

"We are not hamsters, honey, we are registered ham radio operators," he corrects her, his dignity somewhat offended.

"Well, you're a hamster to me, sweetie," she says gently, butting out her inevitable cigarette. She walks over and rumples his hair. He kisses her on the cheek.

Erv and Frenchie are bosom buddies already. They head into town in the van.

"We want to give this baby a test run," he informs us, as he puts on his Stetson.

"I'll fill 'er up, too. That'll give you and Dilly a little more time to visit," Frenchie adds.

Mom bundles me into an extra sweater, and we trudge about the property. She shows me the little creek out back, the pond, Erv's various wood-working, electronic, and machine shops, the ham radio shack. She tells me they're supposed to head south to New Mexico and Texas for the winter. She's full of excited gardening plans for the spring.

"Maybe you'll run into Edie down South," I joke.

"For her sake, I'd better not," she says, her face going hard.

She and Edie met several years ago in Toronto when I was first ill. They were like creatures from totally different planets. Zero said he felt like we were on a bad episode of "Star Trek."

Mom had been horrified when I told of Edie's behavior over these past hard months. She says, "These are not civilized people, and you don't need them in your life." Edie, for her part, refers to Dilly as being "common."

I tell her about Edie's bitter complaining about Zero's portrayal of his family in his writing.

"From what I've seen and heard, I'd say he was pretty much right on the money," Mom says, laughing.

"In my view," I tell her, "Zero was very kind to them in his writing. For the most part, they really are just a bunch of greedy, mean-spirited drunks, and he transformed them into crazy, interesting characters. They should be forever grateful, because without his tales they're a dull and disagreeable lot."

We sit down in the little gazebo beside the creek. Mom looks away. I realize, after a moment, that she's crying.

"What is it, Mom?" I ask gently. I put my arm around her.

"I'm scared to go south," she says. "What if something happens to you? We'll be on the road a lot. What if they can't locate us?"

"Mom, if something happens, it happens, you don't need to fret about it," I respond. "You've got a life to live and so do I. There will always be a lot of people around to look after me. I've been on my own for most of my life and I really don't need you to care for me now. Good things are happening for you and that makes me very happy. We all should be so lucky to get a second chance. Just go for it! I'll be okay."

"But I want so much to be able to do something," she sobs. "I just feel so helpless."

"Well, we're all doing what we can," I tell her, "and you don't know how reassuring it is for me to see you happy again. No, you just get on with your life. If I do need you, I'll call."

Her tears subside. She wipes her eyes, and helps me to my feet.

Erv and Frenchie pull up in the van. Mom has packed us a big lunch. She hands me a red, spiral-bound notebook.

"It's kind of an act of desperation," she says. "But maybe there's something there that can help."

Back on the road. We hurtle down the mountainside toward the beautiful expanse of the valley.

I flip open the red notebook. She has painstakingly collected hundreds of clippings about AIDS and HIV. Her sources range from *The New England Journal of Medicine* to the supermarket tabloids she reads so religiously. Everything is meticulously dated, some annotated, salient points highlighted in yellow and pink. She's obviously put hundreds of hours of work into this. Her way of trying to help. I don't know whether to laugh or cry.

As usual, Frenchie drives relentlessly as we angle up toward Saskatoon. There are few stops. We're headed for the home of one of my oldest friends, Linette. I called her from Mom's, so she's expecting us.

Linette and I met twenty-five years ago, when I was sixteen. In first-year political science. We've been friends ever since. Twenty-five years. That's a long time. We've had some wild fun together. Seen each other through good times and bad. I need to see her now.

"This has got to be my last stop on this journey, except, of course, for home," I tell Frenchie over lunch. The emotional push and pull of these past days and the incredible pace we've sustained have almost finished me. I feel completely hollowed-out. Battered. "I need to give this all a rest."

The Long Way Home

Despite her escalating predicament, Frenchie asks, "Are you sure there's nowhere else you want to take those ashes?"

Actually, there is. I want to take the ashes to New York City and leave some in all of his favorite places, the beautiful old Broadway theaters he loved, Marie's Crisis, The Five Oaks. But that can wait. I'll be damned if I'm going to share that plan with this madwoman, for fear she'll whirl me away to Manhattan in the middle of the night.

I want to stop here. Catch my breath. This is where I come from. This is where Zero said he always felt most at home. He loved the prairie skies, the silences, the subtle beauties of the land. He loved, as well, the traditions of cooperation and the creative foment engendered by this hard and lovely place. He even loved the cold. Long after we moved east, he returned here again and again. I know he'd be happy to be back once more. Canada had become his country; Saskatchewan, his home.

It's dark when we pull into Linette and Fraser's farmyard. Their youngest child, Minou, has seen us drive up. She throws open the door. "They're here! They're here!" she shouts. She stares at Frenchie's hat in wonder, then dashes back into the house. The Great Dane, Clover, snuffles greedily at Frenchie's crotch, then attempts to lick her face.

"Stay the hell off my leg, you big mutt!" she warns.

Linette bustles out of the house. She's baking something and envelops me in a floury embrace. Fraser appears and hugs me, too, his lean cheek bristly against mine.

"Welcome," he says.

The twins, Daniel and Doriano, thunder down the stairs.

I weep. I'd thought I'd cried this out, but every turn of this journey has brought more tears. I'm reeling with a welter of emotion. The enormous reality of my loss, the sheer magnitude of all the love that surrounds me.

Fraser and Linette lead me into the front room. Frenchie is still

181

fending off Clover's increasingly amorous attentions. She introduces herself to everyone and asks if she can use the phone.

"Of course," says Fraser. "Doriano, show Frenchie the phone."

Linette holds me tightly, as my weeping dissolves into dry, hiccuping sobs.

"Thanks for coming here," she says.

"Thanks for being here," I reply.

Frenchie returns to the front room. She's pale and agitated.

"What is it?" I ask.

"I'm in shit up to my ears," she says. "Gotta get this van home *tout de suite*. Vargas says that if I don't have it back in Toronto within thirty-six hours, my ass is grass." She prowls the room like a junkyard dog.

"The bossman was making a rare office appearance, so he even got on the line," she rages. "He's laying charges if I'm not there Monday morning. I told him to shove it up his ass. Pardon my French." But then she shrugs, losing a bit of her steam. "It is his vehicle, though."

"What are you going to do?" asks Fraser.

"Hit the road. I've got a long way to go before Monday morning," she says. She's obviously excited at the prospect of tearing back across the country in a race against the clock.

I stare at her in disbelief. "You are crazy!" I exclaim.

"You betcha!" she replies enthusiastically.

"Well, hon, I won't be going with you. I've got to stop. Now. Or I'm just going to fall apart. You go, if you have to. I've got my credit card. I'll fly back later next week. That'll still give me a week to get my act together for the celebration."

"You sure, partner?"

"Very sure. I'm in the best of hands here."

"You should stop and have a bite to eat," says Linette.

"No can do," replies Frenchie. "I'll grab something down the pike."

The Long Way Home

"You will not," says Fraser. "You'll sit down here for fifteen minutes, while I whip you up some sandwiches."

She scowls at him a moment, then laughs. "I guess fifteen minutes can't hurt."

In a half hour she's ready to leave. The roads, from here on in, will be very familiar. She's traveled them all in her Fabulous Wineberg Sister days. She leans out the window of the van.

"I hate to abandon you, David."

I laugh. "Well, it wouldn't be the first time, would it? There's certainly no point in you losing your job over this."

"It's not just getting the van back to that toad. I miss my sweet sisters, my two little darlings. Lord knows what kind of nonsense they might be up to without the benefit of my strict moral guidance."

I shake my head. "Lord knows, Frenchie, lord only knows."

She turns on the engine. "Well, sport, I'll see you back in Hogtown. You are one hot babe, David. A real trooper."

"So are you, my sweet. This has been a hell of a journey. Thanks."

She hoots with laughter. "Thanks for what? Abducting you, losing you in a ditch, or just pushing you to the brink of a complete breakdown? Let's face it, pal. You have been in the hands of a crazy person and you are just lucky to be alive."

"All of that is true," I concede. "But I still say thank you."

"Well, you are welcome. It's been a great trip for me. It's nice to know that there's still life in this old beast yet."

"Was there ever any doubt?" I hug her awkwardly through the open window. "Tell Snookums and Searcy that if I can get a flight, I'll be back Thursday sometime. I'll try to call them to confirm."

"I know this sounds funny coming from me, but don't rush yourself, kiddo. There's nothing back home that we can't take care of. Anything that needs you can wait."

"You get some rest," I tell her, though I know I'm just whistling in the wind. "And drive carefully."

LABOUR OF LOVE

"Sure thing, sport. I love you." She guns the engine, anxious to be on her way. "I'm outa here!"

The next four days are exactly what I need. No one pressures me to talk. The kids are in school; their parents are at work. The weather is cool, but the sun shines brightly. The autumn prairie is beautiful. I walk the land, or bundle up and lie for hours on my back in the little orchard near the house.

Zero's been dead less than two weeks. My days are full of memory; my nights full of clear and astonishing dreams. I can taste him, smell him, feel the soft contours of his skin, the hard urgencies of his body. In these dreams, he never speaks, but he touches me often, and his smile never fades.

Fraser, Linette, and the children are warm and respectful. They are family for me, too. Every evening, little Minou curls beside me on the couch and tells me elaborate stories. She asks if I will send her a picture of Zero.

Linette and I use every opportunity to relive our memories and share our terrors and our dreams.

I have a lot of history here, but I don't call any of my other old friends. My life has been too crowded for too long. I need to clear some space in the tangle of my being so I can start to renew.

On my last night, there's a full moon. Linette and I drive out to the banks of the South Saskatchewan River. The river and the hills around are bathed in silver. The sky is full of stars. The air cold and sharp.

On a knoll, the tall grasses and silvered sage waving, I scatter the ashes in a small circle. From here, you can see the prairie rolling to the horizon in every direction. Constellations of farm lights punctuate the distant dark. The lights of Saskatoon, though not directly seen, cast a glow on the northern edge of the sky. The river glitters below. This is a good place for him to be.

The Long Way Home

I work my fingers down among the root tangle of the sod at the center of the circle. I dig a small hole. From my shirt pocket, I take a small blue ceramic heart on a tattered string. I gave it to him last Christmas in a Japanese puzzle box. It lay in the innermost of the boxes with a note that told him he had my heart. He wore it like a talisman around his neck for the rest of his life.

I kiss the heart and place it at the bottom of the depression. I remove the block of serpentine from my pack, and set the stone beside the heart. I carefully refill the hole so the serpentine is nestled in the prairie earth. Barely protruding from the soil, it seems like it's been there forever.

Linette stands quietly behind me. I turn and take her hand.

"Let's go."

I've managed to catch the red-eye home. I sit in my window seat somewhere over Manitoba. In search of a pen, I unsnap my jacket pocket. Linette has filled my pockets with prairie sage. I crush some leaves between my fingers and inhale their wild moon-drenched magic. Loco weed. I'm anxious to be home.

I don't have money for bus or cab fare from the airport and didn't call anyone to pick me up. I do have a transit token, so I take the bus to the subway and head for home. It's still very early and the car is virtually empty. The escalator at the Wellesley station is out of order. I trudge up the stairs with my bag. I stop for a moment by the turnstiles to catch my breath.

Searcy and Snookums are outside the station. Electioneering. Snookums is handing out flyers. His head, bare of either turban or toupee, shines in the morning light. A huge poster is propped against the wall. The poster features a performance shot of Searcy, arms flung out dramatically, eyes glistening, glamorous, mouth open wide in

song. Across the bottom in blazing orange script it proclaims—
GOLDBERG—NO MORE SHIT!

The candidate is working the morning rush hour. He bobs and
weaves in the crush of the crowd. Shakes hands. Curtsies to some,
hugs others. He creates a carnival atmosphere. Some recoil in outrage;
most seem pleased to see him.

Three towering young men in University of Toronto Varsity
Blues basketball jackets shoulder through the station door. "No more
shit!" exclaims the tallest. "Right on!"

I catch Snookums's eye. His eyes widen in amazement. He
immediately slips in to join me. Kisses me on both cheeks, then hard
on the mouth. "*Quelle* surprise, precious!" he enthuses. "Where have
you been?"

"Just about everywhere," I say wearily. "It's a long, long story.
Too long for here."

"You will tell it, though?" he pleads.

"You can bet on that," I promise him, "but later."

He puts his arm around me. "Are you okay, precious?" he asks
tenderly.

I manage a tired smile. "More or less."

We watch Searcy for a moment.

"He's good at this," I marvel.

"Yes, precious, and I think he just might win," Snookums confides. "They love him."

Searcy finally sees us and rushes in. He hugs me. Then he
scrutinizes me at arm's length. "You look like you're about to collapse," he informs me. "You go right on home. Leave your bag here
with us. We'll bring it over as soon as we've finished here. There's
fresh-ground coffee ready to go. Just turn on the machine.

"There's lots and lots of mail. And the phone has been ringing
constantly. Everyone who ever knew Zero, and many who didn't."

"And, of course, many, many messages from the beautiful

Lance," adds Snookums. "I've had to clear the tape several times a day."

I head east on Wellesley. I'll pick up some groceries on my way back to the house. At Pusateri's, I start to fill a bag with peaches. Two tiny older women are pinching at the nectarines beside me. They look like little withered children in camel hair coats.

"Did you see that ruckus at the subway?" asks one.

"That nice Mr. Goldberg?" replies the other. "He's already got my vote."

"Isn't that interesting," the first responds.

They turn to each other and in unison declare, "No more shit!" Totally shocked at their own boldness, they collapse against each other, giggling wildly.

I let myself in the front door. I switch on the coffee maker, immediately comforted by its familiar thumping gurgle and the heady aroma of the fresh-ground brew.

A pile of mail spills across the kitchen table. A letter from Lance is on top. I pick it up. Put it down. It feels like good news. The answering machine is frantic with messages. On a pad beside the phone Snookums has recorded all previous calls.

I pour my coffee and wander through the house. I keep expecting to hear his voice. For him to step into the hallway. To feel his arms slip around me. But, no, he's truly gone. There is a different quality to the emptiness around me. Every room resonates with his absence. And yet I feel him everywhere. Palpable. Real. Maybe too real.

The evidence of this terrible summer is all about me. The catheters, the diaper supply, wheelchair, commode, the support bars clamped to bathtub and bathroom walls, the dressings, the hospital bed. I remind myself to call Home Care. I want all of this gone. I want him back.

LABOUR OF LOVE

There is a tentative knock at the door. It pulls me back from my reverie. I'm exasperated by the interruption. "Who is it?" I bark.

"It's only that nuisance, Searcy Goldberg. Please let me in," he sings out in a high, fluting child's voice. "Please, Mr. David, I shall only stay a moment, if you'll only let me in."

I fling open the door. "You sound like some sort of incubus trying to lure me out of my little home, so you can devour me. You make me feel like I'm trapped in some ghastly tale from the Brothers Grimm!" I rant.

He shushes me, finger to his lips. "I've brought your bag as promised," he says, reverting to the rich contralto of his real voice, never once stopping for a breath. "I've been so worried about you. But I really won't stay. I've already talked to Frenchie. Your version can wait. Though, as you well know, I am dying for the details. Snookums sends apologies. Crisis at the magazine. We'll both be by with dinner later in the day. Is six o'clock okay? Until then put your feet up, read the mail, check your messages, chill out, and maybe even try to get some rest. See you at six. Ta!" He puts down my bag, blows me a kiss, pirouettes down the stairs, and is already making a very grand and regal progress west on Maitland by the time I've caught my breath enough to speak.

I sit down at the kitchen table and begin to sort the mail. There are the inevitable bills, theater flyers, fast-food pitches, assorted other junk. There's a lurid invitation to the premiere of Randy's movie. It's finally going to open at the Festival of Festivals later in the fall. I and a guest are invited to a reception following the screening. RSVP. I catch myself thinking that Zero's sure going to be pissed off to miss this one.

Mostly though, they are heartfelt message of sorrow and love for Zero and myself. But this is too hard right now. I push the remaining unread cards and letters into a neat stack. They can wait.

I do open one from Edie. She has clipped the Arkansas obituaries and sent a copy of Farley's homily as well. I give them only a cursory scan. Closer scrutiny will just make me angry. I set them aside, too.

I slit open Lance's letter. It's bulky, full of immigration forms, pressed flowers, lipstick kisses on scraps of paper, and a note scribbled on several pages torn from an exercise book.

I read it slowly, savoring. He's been to the consulate and they assured him that there should be no problem. His spouse need only make application for him from Canada. They say he could be here to stay by Christmas. In the meantime he can even visit. Maybe he can be here for Zero's celebration. He wants me to call him tonight. And I will. He loves me very much.

I'm dizzy with all this. Lance. I can't believe he may finally be on his way. To stay. That maybe this time I'll actually get to keep him. It overwhelms me that he loves me enough to do this. How can I let someone love me so much in the state I'm in? With no guarantees of time. How can I not?

It's a risk. A gamble for us both. There is no safe way to be in love. There are no condoms for the heart.

I check the messages on the phone.

Mary Bull declares herself a soon-to-be Broadway sensation. Her show will open in Boston in a week. If it's humanly possible, she'll be here on the October long weekend for the celebration.

Jesus Las Vegas has called on behalf of Zero's Uncle Marcus and, of course, himself. Marcus is devastated by Zero's death, but is in complete traction again, swathed in bandages from head to toe, immobile and unable to speak. Earlier this spring while being honored by a grateful Florida for his contribution to the culture of the state, Marcus had tumbled into the orchestra pit in the final gala number of the evening. He has broken nearly every bone in his body. Jesus Las Vegas soldiers on, tending to Marcus, running the dinner theater empire and appearing seven evenings a week as the star of the long-running country-and-western hit musical, *Gimme Back My Pork-chop*. He'll call back when he has more time to talk.

189

LABOUR OF LOVE

* * *

The phone rings. Against my better judgment I answer.

"You're finally home. I was worried sick! Well, where have y'all been?" cries Edie. "Just thought I'd call and check on how y'all were comin' with the will."

Will this never end? "Listen, Edie, I've been away, I'm completely worn out, and I don't want to talk to you right now, particularly about Zero's will. I will send you a copy of the will as soon as it goes through probate. Now is there anything else?"

"Yes, I wanted to thank you. We had a lovely little ceremony to inter the cremains that you sent. I was very sorry that you couldn't be here with us. Absolutely everyone was asking about you."

"Uh-huh," I say. I have no patience with this.

"Did y'all get the obituaries I sent you?" she chirps. "I sent along the homily my cousin, Farley Potts, delivered. I think it's very beautiful. It brought tears to every eye." She begins to sob loudly, out of control. "He would have loved it."

I've had it. "What a crock! Listen, Edie, you've whitewashed Zero's life completely in those things. He never wanted that kind of carrying on. He left explicit instructions that that shouldn't happen. He'd be outraged at how you disregarded his last wishes.

"I know you needed to do something. Something to help you through the grief I'm sure you feel. I don't begrudge you that. I only wish you had taken the time to know your son while he was alive, and respected his wishes when he died. Now you can go on and live with your delusions and the lies you've fabricated about him and his life. But I just don't want to hear about it anymore. And no, I'm not going to praise you and your beloved Farley for those sanitized rewrites of Zero's life. No AIDS, no real acknowledgment of his wonderful life, his gayness, his vital friends and relationships, the courage and creativity of his work."

190

The Long Way Home

She's got her tears more or less under control. "Well, I guess y'all never expected anything more from us."

"Nor anything less."

"I think y'all forget just how provincial we are here in Arkansas," she sniffs.

"Edie," I reply, "that is something I never forget."

She hangs up.

The phone rings again immediately. I know it's her. This time, though, it's different. She's crying softly. "I'm sorry, David. I am so sorry. Please don't cut me out of your life. I need to be able to talk to y'all. Y'all are the only link I have to most of my son's life. The only living person who can possibly begin to share some understanding of my grief. We've restarted this friendship before, we can do it again," she pleads.

Her voice is so full of delusion, so very, very bleak and lonely, I know that if she'd been here, face-to-face, my instinct would have been to try somehow to make it all better.

I ache for her sorrow at this moment. She is so unhappy. But this needs to stop. I tell her so. "Edie, I promise that anything Zero has designated for you in his will will be sent as soon as it's humanly possible. Now I'm going to hang up and I hope never to hear from you again. I will not answer calls or open letters. As of now, I consider all business with you to be over."

She's sobbing harder now. "I need to be your friend, David, please."

"And I need to stay alive. You know, Edie, it's four years ago tonight that I was first being wheeled into emergency. They didn't think I'd make it through the night. But I did. And I'm still here. And I intend to stay here for a while."

Unable to stop herself, she reverts to form. With a bitter laugh, she exclaims, "Well, you'll be very lucky to get another year, won't you now!"

LABOUR OF LOVE

I am so tired of all this. It just never ends. "It's simply too late, Edie. I'm sorry. This has all just hurt too much. Good-bye."

I think she finally realizes that I'm serious. In a sad small voice, muffled by tears, she replies, "Good-bye, David."

It's the first time in all these many years that she hasn't hung up on me. The first time she's ever bothered to actually say good-bye.

I set the receiver gently in its cradle and unplug the phone.

I take the pad on which Snookums has recorded phone messages and head outside to the garden. I settle in my favorite chair beneath the Siberian olive.

The garden looks a little the worse for wear. But the yellow hibiscus on the deck is covered in blooms. A couple of finches burble their bubbling song from their singing perch on the edge of the deck before winging up and away to roughhouse among the scarlet berries at the top of the mountain ash.

I flip through the pad. There are scores of messages. For the most part they are like the mail messages I've already set aside. These, too, can wait.

At the end of them all, Snookums has written in his florid scrawl, "Remember," then underneath in point form, "Stay angry," "Keep laughing," and "Never stop loving." I lean back in my chair and take a deep breath. I close my eyes.

Hundreds of bickering starlings suddenly settle on the power lines and bushes in the back. They are loud. Raucous. Alive.

I reread Snookums's message. Stay angry. Keep laughing. Never stop loving.

"Yes," I whisper to Zero, to myself, to our home, to the garden, to the world, "I can do that."